TANK'S CHOICE

E J Davis

D0996223

CHRISTIAN FOCUS PUBLICATIONS

Published by
Christian Focus Publications, Geanies House,
Fearn, Tain, Ross-shire, IV20 1TW, Scotland, with
kind permission by Openbook Publishers
© Openbook Publishers
Text copyright © E J Davis
Inside illustrations by Ron Lisle

Cover design by Donna Macleod
Cover illustration by Jack McCarthy, Pinkbarge

ISBN 1-85792-102-X

Printed and bound in Great Britain by Cox &
Wyman Ltd, Reading, Berks

Chapter 1

'You've got a choice. You can either come with us to Gran's, or you can go to the youth-group camp with Jarryn', Mum said.

Tank looked out the window. He didn't really want to do either of those things. Gran's was OK for a day, but three days was a bit too much. And the youth-group camp . . . well, it would be great if it wasn't a 'Christian' youth group. Jarryn had asked him to come weeks ago, and Tank still hadn't given him an answer. Now it looked as if his time was up and the pressure was on for a reply.

Mum's pressure was, anyway — Jarryn had only asked once, and very carefully at that, but Tank knew that Jarryn needed to know by Friday so that he could tell the organisers. The trouble was, there were no other options. Already he had held off giving an answer for as long as possible in the hope that some other opportunity would crop up and save him, but it hadn't. Tank had a fatalistic suspicion, however, that the moment he did commit himself to either one or the other of his options, some never-to-be-repeated alternative would show up immediately and leave him tearing his hair out with frustration.

The decision could not be put off any longer, however. Mum wanted an answer. Gran's, a little house in town, nothing to do but watch TV, weed the garden, or clean out the shed . . .

Or the youth group. Well, maybe, except they would all be singing and praying and doing whatever Christians did. He'd feel a real dork, and not just for himself either. He would

3

feel a dork for *them* too! He hated feeling embarrassed on other people's behalf, but when they started talking to thin air like that . . . How on earth could they be sure anyone was there? And they all *looked* such dorks when they did that, it just chewed him all up inside.

Still, some of the program looked OK. Abseiling, bushwalking, and everything. Maybe he could just disappear when the silly bits were on. 'OK, I'll go to the youth-group camp with Jarryn', he finally said.

'Well, about time too', Mum sighed. 'You'd better ring and tell him so that he can book your place.'

Tank climbed heavily to his feet. 'Yeah, I guess so.'

Jarryn put down the phone receiver with mixed feelings. Tank was coming on the youth-group camp. It was what he'd been praying for, yet he found it very discomforting. Secretly, he realised, he'd been hoping that Tank wouldn't come. It was six months since he'd first told Tank about becoming a Christian, and Tank's reaction had been so intense that it had nearly finished their friendship. Now, Tank was coming to a *Christian* camp. He'd meet kids he didn't know, and have to join in on activities so alien to him he'd probably blow a fuse, and on top of that . . . Well, Jarryn could just imagine what some of the camp program would look like through Tank's eyes. He wished Tank was a Christian already, and he wished even harder that God wouldn't use him, Jarryn, to reach Tank, that God would use someone else. But it seemed more and more to Jarryn that using him to reach Tank was *exactly* what God had in mind, and Jarryn didn't like it one bit.

There were a few bonuses, as it turned out. To begin with, because the camp was in the Gawler Ranges, which started at the boundaries of their farms, Tank and Jarryn were allowed to take the old Landcruiser and drive themselves out. And for Tank there was the added reassurance that he was not the only non-Christian who was going. It seemed there were a number who had been invited along, and he received this news outwardly with an offhand shrug but inwardly with a great sigh of relief.

The Landcruiser loaded and fuelled, and their gear packed and strapped down, they set off eagerly, hoping to arrive at roughly the same time as the other campers. A long stretch of track reached out before them. Puddled from recent rains, it alternately encouraged their progress and then retarded it. Hummocks in the road lifted and dropped them, potholes jarred them, and clay-based puddles caused them to slide all over the place until their tyres grabbed onto firmer ground again. From time to time washaways, where streaming rainwater had channelled little gullies off the road and into the sandy soil beside it, gaped up blackly at them. Clouds vied with sunshine, and a healthy breeze knocked and buffeted the vehicle as they drove.

'Hope it doesn't rain', Tank commented a little gloomily.

Jarryn squinted up through the window, almost resting his chin on the steering wheel. 'Shouldn't', he said. 'The forecast said it was supposed to clear up.'

The shearers' quarters at Mount Lever station consisted of two rows of little iron huts, a long stone room with a fire at one end surrounded by a varied assortment of settees, lounge chairs, and seats, and an enormous dining room and kitchen area. There was a shower block at the far end of the sleeping quarters with three huge showers, and behind the kitchen, some little distance away, was a small generator hut.

Tank stood outside the kitchen door and stared down the slope toward the shearing shed some five hundred metres away. Beyond that and to the right, a vast plain of bluebush and grassland rolled away for kilometres before rising again on distant hillsides. To the left rose the first hefty, granite-strewn feet of a range of mountains. Turning slowly to his feet, his eyes followed the line of mountain tops around until he faced the kitchen, and then moved up and up to a point that must surely be the highest of any mountains around.

Further views of anything beyond were effectively blocked here, and Tank felt an urge to climb to the top, just to see what was on the other side, but already cars and utes and trailers were pulling up on the granite gravelled area in front of the sleeping quarters and people were spilling out everywhere. Kids and adults, some strangers and some Tank knew from school, all laughing and exclaiming, greeting one another as if they hadn't just travelled 60 k's together but instead had not seen each other for months. Tank hated the beginnings and ends of camps.

'Let's grab a room', Jarryn suggested. His eyes were bright with excitement, and already he was enjoying himself. Lots of people called out to him, and Jarryn grinned broadly in reply or waved or called back. He was obviously quite at home in this company, and Tank felt more than a twinge of irritation that he was here for no other reason than that there had only been two options to choose from: here or Gran's. Feeling disgruntled, he turned to the Landcruiser and grabbed his swag, hauling it out so roughly that he nearly dropped it, and followed Jarryn into one of the huts.

Two wooden steps led up into the little room. A layer of fine red dust crunched underfoot as Tank walked to one of the two beds and dumped his swag on the grim, uncovered mattress. A puff of red cloud shot out from it as the swag landed. The bed creaked stiffly. A wooden frame like a cupboard without doors was fixed against one wall to store things in, a bony chair of bleached wood squatted between the beds, and a brilliant green wardrobe with a full-length mirror glared back from next to the door. There was nothing else in the room except a single bare globe light which, when Tank flicked the switch, refused to turn on.

'Needs the generator, I suppose', Jarryn grinned.

'Yeah.'

'Come on, we'd better get that food unpacked and into the kitchen, or we might not get tea.'

Kitchens to Tank were just kitchens — that was until he saw the Mount Lever shearers' kitchen. It was huge! An enormous wood stove, already belching out smoke, dominated half of one wall. Facing it, on the opposite wall, stood two gas stoves. A wooden table in the middle stood stoutly among cartons, eskies, boxes, bags, bottles, crates, and hampers. Mrs Woods was organising and Mrs Paige was sorting, while some kids carted things in and out, and others explored the cupboards, the mouse-proof pantry, the kerosene fridges, and the sink.

'We'll need some wood, you boys, to get the hot-water system going', Mrs Paige suggested, as she relieved Tank of his esky. 'Go out that way and see if you can get the fire going.' She gestured toward another door leading out of the kitchen.

It led to a little veranda. Beyond this was a large corrugated-iron water tank resting on brick supports, and underneath it were definite signs of old fires. Jarryn moved past Tank and headed for a patch of scrub some hundred metres away, where he began picking up old branches.

Tank squatted down and peered underneath the water tank. Piles of ashes crept up the sides of the support walls, which were black with soot. Someone had left an old newspaper under a stone by the wall, so Tank began screwing up the pages and throwing them in, well back, so that the fire would be centred underneath the water tank. With a long, stout branch he raked clumsily at the accumulated ashes, pulling them forward so that they could later be shovelled away. It was while he was working hard at this that he heard the kitchen screen door bang shut and the sound of foot-steps coming lightly toward him.

Sitting back on his heels he turned and looked, focusing first on a pair of trendy Reeboks. Then he saw a pair of brilliant green socks, rolled-up jeans, a slender waist sporting a brightly coloured stretchy belt with a butterfly buckle and a yellow, red, and green windcheater, tucked in, and finally the most amazing face he had ever seen in his life.

He consciously made himself close his mouth. She was *gorgeous*! She had pale skin, pink cheeks, a cute nose, and the hugest, most glorious green eyes he had ever seen. Even under all the make-up she wore, he decided, there was something special about that face. And to top it all, there were masses and masses of red-gold hair, looping and bouncing around her face.

'G'day, short stuff', the girl teased, looking down at him. Feeling a mixture of superiority, because he knew for sure that one thing he *wasn't* was short, and embarrassment because she'd spoken to him, he stood up. She grinned as he stood. 'O well, not so short, then', she said. 'What are you doing?'

'Lighting a fire', Tank answered simply, still uncomfortable.

Jarryn returned then with an armful of kindling. 'G'day', he said to the girl as he passed them and began to juggle the wood onto the newspaper that Tank had put into the fire pit.

'G'day, yourself', the girl said, watching him. 'Where are you guys from?'

'Our folks have farms about an hour's drive from here, that way', Tank said, pointing. 'Where are you from?'

'Coffin Bay', she answered. 'I'm Scarlet', she added with a screwed-up face, 'Scarlet Tekker'.

'I'm Jarryn McEvan', said Jarryn as he stood up. 'You got matches?' he asked Tank.

Tank fumbled in his pockets and produced a box of matches. 'And I'm Peter King, but most people call me Tank', he said, handing the box to Jarryn.

9

Jarryn turned back to the fire. Tank couldn't take his eyes off Scarlet.

'Well, Tank, Jarryn, it's been nice meeting you. I'll be seeing you around, OK?' and with that she smiled cutely at them and turned back to the kitchen. Tank blew a sibilant whistle. 'Wow!' he said.

Jarryn stood up and backed away from the clouds of smoke which were now billowing out from the fire pit and threatening to smoke him alive. He turned to Tank and grinned broadly. 'Yeah, not too bad at all', he agreed.

Good humour suddenly restored, Tank grinned back. 'I guess we'd better get some stumps, or this fire will die out before the chill's even left the water', he said, and together they set off for the scrub again.

Chapter 2

Right from the beginning it was obvious that things weren't going to be allowed to dawdle. Within the hour everyone had picked their rooms, dumped their gear inside, and unloaded the food, and they were getting together in the 'lounge' hut. Scarlet was already there, along with a tall girl with a broad smile and long hair.

Tank and Jarryn grabbed a seat each and sat down. Gradually the room filled until everyone was there. Andrew Woods called for quiet. 'Well, I'd just like to welcome everyone first of all, especially those people who haven't been to one of our camps before. We hope that you get lots out of it. I'd also like to welcome Mr Steven Barrow, our camp speaker.'

Steven must have been nearly two metres tall, and was lean as a beanpole, fair-haired, tanned, and blue-eyed. He was, Tank guessed, probably about thirty-five years old, and looked as if he could handle anything from a surfboard to a bucking brumby. 'He's the one who does the abseiling', Jarryn whispered. Tank nodded.

'Thank you, Andrew', Steven said, 'and thank you everyone for inviting me here for this camp. Some terrific things are going to happen around here in the next few days, I think, and I hope everyone's going to learn a lot too. What's more, I really believe that no-one will leave this camp unchanged in some way, even if it's in just a very small way.'

There was a silence as everyone digested this. Tank felt that barrier creeping up again — he didn't want anything to do with anything 'Christianic', as he called it. But he needn't

11

have worried now, because Steven wasn't about to begin a sermon. The man smiled. 'We've got lots planned — bush walks, spotlighting, talks, abseiling, chasing goats if we can find them, mountain climbing and lots more — but before all that, I think we should have tea.'

A great explosion of agreement met with this suggestion, and everyone began to file out of the lounge room.

During tea a lot of the 'housekeeping' rules were explained. The campers were to be divided up into groups, all of which would take turns at cooking, washing dishes, cleaning the showers and toilets, or collecting wood to keep the fires in the wood stove and hot-water systems going. Jarryn and Tank were both delighted to find themselves in the same group as Scarlet and her friend Gemma. Their first duty turned out to be dishes.

After making a beautiful ugly face, Scarlet set about organising everyone. The three other people in their duty group she told to clear the tables, Gemma was quickly placed at the sink to wash, and Jarryn and Tank , tea-towels in hand, waited by the draining-board.

'What are *you* going to do?' Jarryn asked in mock outrage.

'Oh, just sit here and look good', Scarlet answered airily, as she sprang neatly onto the huge wooden table.

Jarryn's eyebrows rose a little at that, but what could he say? There was no doubt that she did look good, so who was he to argue? But he couldn't get over her actually saying it. She sure wasn't shy!

'She can put the dishes away', Tank said, stepping in. He wanted to add: 'and still look good doing it', but he wasn't game enough, and to her credit Scarlet did put most of the dishes away, although probably not where they belonged.

Dishes finished, they made their way back to the lounge, where Adrian was just announcing that a night walk would be leaving in 15 minutes for those people who wanted to join in.

'Shall we go?' Tank asked Jarryn.

Jarryn grinned. 'You bet, we might spook a goat or something.'

'I think I'll get my torch', Tank grinned.

The track past the shearing shed crossed a ramp and then rolled on downhill toward the plain beyond. There was an almost full moon up, and millions of stars frosted the now clear sky. In clumps and small groups, torches flickering, the night walkers made their way toward a black mound in the distance. Tank looked for Scarlet and heard rather than saw her, some little distance ahead, giggling with some friends. The night air was brittle with cold, and Tank was sure there would be a frost by morning; right now, though, walking was making him warm.

Halfway between the shearing shed, which could now be distinguished only in vague silhouette form against the kitchen lights behind it, and the dark lump of starlessness in front of them that was the first small mountain of that part of the range, they came to a creek. It was dry, but cut so deep into the sandy soil that it must have been well worth seeing when it ran. After that, the ground began to rise, steadily getting steeper and steeper as it approached the mountain. By now the group was spread out, as everyone clambered

13

upward. It hadn't looked this steep from the shearing shed! Huge boulders as big as kitchen tables and refrigerators and cars rested against one another, cemented by spear grass, wattle bushes, prickles, and dead branches. The seemingly gentle little mountain was much more rugged close up than it had looked from the distance.

Jarryn and Tank, however, were not put off by this, and raced each other to see who could climb the highest. Granite boulders were sometimes helpful, but the smaller loose stones and gravel were treacherously unstable. Several times rocks gave way underfoot or gravel would slide beneath them, so that they sometimes had to sit down or grab a nearby tree branch to regain their balance, but it was all part of the challenge.

'Are we near the top yet?' Tank wanted to know when they paused for breath.

'No, there's miles to go yet', Jarryn told him. Tank groaned.

'Don't tell me you're tired', Scarlet's voice teased as she pushed her way toward them through some wattles. Gemma followed behind her, puffing softly.

'No way', Jarryn said. 'We're just waiting for you.'

'Ah yeah', Scarlet agreed sarcastically. Jarryn grinned.

'At least you two have got torches', Gemma said. 'I thought we were only going along the track, and didn't bring mine.'

'You can share ours', Tank offered, secretly delighted at being able to offer help in such a way that meant Scarlet would then stay nearby.

'OK, but I still want to go to the top', Scarlet said.

'Me too', Tank replied. 'You coming, Jarryn?'

Jarryn looked at Gemma. She was still breathless and didn't really seem very keen about going much further, yet he felt he couldn't just go and leave her on her own. There were other people around, but it would be difficult to recognise who they were in the dark. 'We'll follow on behind for a while', he said finally. 'You go on. We'll meet you on the way back.'

'Right', Scarlet agreed happily. 'C'mon, you great lump. I'll race you.'

They were gone in three steps, swallowed up by the blackness and the scrub and the mountain. Jarryn looked across at Gemma, who was sitting on a dustbin-sized boulder, still a little out of breath.

'If you want to go with them, I'll be fine', she said to Jarryn. 'I can wait here till I get my breath back, and then head down again.'

'No, it's OK. I won't be able to see anything from the top, anyway; it's too dark.'

Gemma nodded. 'I'm afraid I'm not very fit', she laughed. 'I had to have my appendix out not very long ago, and it's left me weaker than I thought.'

Jarryn was surprised. 'Does Scarlet know?' he asked.

Gemma looked down at her shoes, obviously a little uncomfortable. 'Yes', she said, 'but I didn't let on that I was finding it hard. I really want her to enjoy this camp . . .'

There was a pause. Jarryn wondered if Gemma was a Christian too. Perhaps she was trying to reach her friend, just as he was trying to reach Tank. 'Have you been on camps like this before?' he asked.

'Yes. Steven Barrow is our local youth-group leader and a lay reader at our church. We came with him.'

'And you asked Scarlet to come with you?' Jarryn asked.

'Yes.'

'I asked Tank to come', he said, but he just couldn't bring himself to add what he was hoping might happen as a result. 'Are you feeling any better?' he asked.

Gemma looked up. She might have smiled, but Jarryn couldn't see in the dark. 'Yes, much better now I've got my breath back, thanks.'

'We may as well head down again then. The others'll catch up with us when they're ready.'

Gemma stook up. 'Thanks', she said a little awkwardly, 'for waiting, I mean'.

''S OK', Jarryn grinned. ' I'll get you back for it somehow. You go first, and I'll shine the torch.'

For all his long-leggedness, general fitness, and not inconsiderable strength, Tank was having a hard time staying ahead of Scarlet. She was as nimble as a mountain goat and quick to spot access between rocks, or through trees, even without a torch. Often she was level with him, or even ahead, and on those occasions when she was behind him he could sense her impatience as she waited for him to get through to clearer ground.

In some ways he was pleased that Jarryn hadn't come, but in others he wished that he was here. At least Jarryn would have taken the pressure off Tank to make conversation. Right now, Tank's mind had totally dried up of anything to say at all. To cover up, he just concentrated on climbing.

16

The mountain was no gentle hill. It was steep, prickly, and insecure, and the top, or the total black outline of it against the starlit sky, did not seem to be getting much closer. Step after step he continued, his breathing heavy, his legs aching. He could hear Scarlet's equally heavy breathing next to him at the moment, as she climbed beside him, sharing what the torchlight revealed ahead. She showed no sign of slowing down, though.

Presently the torchlight picked up a path. 'Goat track', Tank muttered, and turned onto it. Scarlet said nothing, but dropped into place behind him, and they followed the track. It made the going a little easier, but also longer, as it seemed to be wandering more across the mountain than up to its summit, but they were still climbing. At times they had to get down on their hands and knees to crawl under scrubby bushes; at other times it was easier to detour and climb over the rocks, then rejoin the track further along, than to try to jump where the goats obviously jumped.

Finally they came out onto a cleared area, totally bare of any vegetation at all. Grudgingly the mountain admitted they'd reached its bald summit.

A cold breeze blew, and to enjoy it Scarlet took off her jumper and tied it around her waist. Tank did the same, and then sat down on the bare pebbles to regain his breath. Sweat was running down his neck and back, and his heart pounded in his chest. There wasn't very much to see, however. A black silhouette horizon of other mountain tops blocked out the star-shine of the sky. Below that, no detail was visible at all, except, far away in the distance, the lights of the shearers' quarters where they were camping. No-one else, it seemed, had ventured to the very top of the mountain. There was just Scarlet and himself, and for a moment Tank was tongue-tied.

'That was great!' Scarlet exclaimed, still breathless.

'Yeah', Tank agreed.

Scarlet sat a little distance from him on an esky-sized rock surrounded with pebbles. 'Why is it so bare?' she asked.

Tank shone the torch around, illuminating barren rocks, empty, rock-strewn areas, and one or two stark, charred, tree skeletons. 'Must have been a fire up here', he said. 'Sometimes lightning starts fires.'

'An act of God?' Scarlet said, a slightly challenging note creeping into her voice.

'No way! Just lightning. It just happens!' Tank replied, and then wondered if he'd said too much.

'You're not one of these Christians, then?' Scarlet asked.

Tank looked over at her, but he couldn't see her face. It was hard to gauge just what she meant. Where did she stand, anyway? Was she a Christian, or was she just along for some other reason, like him?

'No', he said simply.

'Me neither', she replied.

Tank was suddenly very interested in why she was here if she wasn't a Christian, but he couldn't bring himself to ask.

He didn't need to. 'I came with Gemma', she said. 'She's been asking me to come on one of these camps for ages, and I've run out of excuses. It sounded all right except for the churchy bits, so I said OK.'

'I know what you mean. I might just fade away somewhere when they start that sort of thing', Tank said.

'I might just fade with you', Scarlet agreed.

Tank was delighted at this. He stood up. 'I guess we should get back', he said. 'Jarryn will be wondering where I've got to.'

Scarlet stood up too. 'And Gemma's probably having kittens worrying about me. Besides, I could use a drink.'

'Here, you take the torch. I'll follow you down', Tank said, handing it over. Taking it, Scarlet set off cheerfully back down the mountain side.

Someone had just lit a fire. As they crossed the ramp, Jarryn and Gemma could see its bright flames flickering about in the middle of the grassy area in front of the sleeping quarters. There was no real glow yet, but the flames illuminated the dark twig shapes as they danced around, lighting up first this part then another part. Jarryn decided it was going to be a good fire when it took hold. Already most of the campers were collecting around it, alternately warming their backs then their fronts, like rotisseried chickens, constantly turning in front of the growing heat.

'I'm going to get an extra jumper', Gemma said, and headed off for her room. Jarryn made for the kitchen, where he found a huge cup and filled it to the top with water from the rainwater tank outside. He was just starting his second cupful when Tank arrived.

'Hurry up, I'm as dry as a desert', he stirred.

Jarryn grinned and threw the last of the water over Tank before handing him the cup. 'Did you get to the top?' Jarryn asked.

19

'Yeah. Couldn't see much, though, it was too dark. We'll have to go back in daylight for a better look. There's been a fire up there; nothing's growing at all. What's happening now?'

'Don't know. I think everyone's getting together outside by the fire.'

Tank drained his cup, tossed the last drops in Jarryn's direction, and turned back into the kitchen. 'Wonder if there's anything to eat?' he said.

'We get supper later', Jarryn told him.

'Good. Let's get back to the fire, then.'

By the time Jarryn and Tank arrived back at the fire, everyone was there and someone had a guitar out. They found a place to sit on one of the rugs someone had spread out, and were soon clapping along to 'Click Go the Shears'. They sang a lot, mostly well-known songs, some pop stuff, and some Christian choruses that Tank, in his present good humour, didn't seem to mind at all. Jarryn was feeling nervous, nonetheless. In probability someone would give a talk, or, at the very least, say prayers, and on Tank's behalf Jarryn dreaded the thought of it. What would Tank do? If he was really angry about it, he'd storm off and not worry who might be offended in the process. In his mind, Jarryn began to pray.

As it turned out, Tank didn't do anything. He had already half guessed that there would probably be some sort of talk before everyone went to bed, and had decided that there really wasn't very much he could do about it at this stage. After all, it was a *Christian* youth-group camp and this was what they *did*, so it would be pretty stupid to walk out in the middle of a talk. Far better to find out the program first and organise himself to be missing when the future talks were scheduled. Having decided this, Tank was quite relaxed when the guitarist finished the song he was playing and Steven began to speak. Tank's eyes searched out Scarlet across the fire, and he rolled his eyes when he found her watching him. She smiled beautifully in return, and his spirits soared.

Steven spoke about the program first, explaining that the mornings were to be set aside for Christian study sessions, the afternoons for activities such as abseiling or bushwalking, and the evenings for a get-together, fun and games, and then a prayer time before bed. Having set out the program, he then spoke about what the study sessions would cover.

Tank wasn't really interested. He kept stealing glances at Scarlet, hoping like mad that she would look back at him and smile again. A couple of times she did, and Tank was so wrapped up in this new wonderful excitement that he wasn't even hearing Steven at all. After a while, however, he realised that Scarlet's attention was caught. What was it that Steven was saying that had her interested? Tank tuned in. It was something about choices — choices between truth and lies, and how the whole world was a mixture of truth and lies, and that Jesus would reveal the truth to those who wanted it. God didn't force people to believe in him, but he was waiting, giving them a *choice* . . .

Steven continued: 'The Bible tells us that Jesus offers us all a new and fulfilling life, as it's meant to be. He knows and cares for each of us, and he wants us to acknowledge him as Lord. He is standing knocking at our doors, waiting. It's up to us, though, to allow him in.'

21

There was a moment's silence.

'That's the truth, but the choice is still up to you. Tomorrow we'll look into this question of truth in more detail. For now, though, I'm ready for some supper.'

A general approval rippled through the campers, and people began to stand up and move toward the kitchen again. Tank stood up and looked over to Scarlet, but she was already moving away toward her hut with Gemma. It didn't look as if he'd see her any more tonight. He turned to Jarryn. 'I'm starving', he said. 'You coming up for some supper?'

Jarryn nodded and grinned a reply, taking off for the kitchen at a run, Tank hard on his heels behind him.

Chapter 3

For some silly reason, everyone in the entire camp was up and about before seven o'clock the following morning. Jarryn's duty group was in charge of cleaning up toilets and showers, which meant that they had to wait until after everyone was finished first. Tank and Jarryn filled in the time by flicking the remaining embers of the fire together and poking a few half-burnt, outlying twigs onto them to get it flaming again. As the twigs began to catch, and twisting ribbons of smoke writhed and curled upward in the still frosty air, Tank looked toward the mountain they had climbed the night before. The top, he could now see, was indeed bald. It looked like a roundish pate, with a fringe of hair half slipped sideways, then dribbling down in an elongated drip into the scrub below. Tank wondered why he hadn't noticed it yesterday.

For all the noise the breakfast duty group were making in the kitchen and the other campers in their rooms behind them, it felt peaceful and calm by the fire. The twigs had crackled to flame, and as he watched them Tank wrestled with what he was going to tell Jarryn about his intentions to miss the morning talk.

Jarryn wandered off to find more dead wood from some nearby scrub, and when he came back Tank still hadn't decided what to say. Part of the reason for this was that he hadn't caught up with Scarlet yet. He hadn't seen her at all, but judging by the squeals and giggles coming from the direction of the showers he had a pretty good idea where she was. Would she still fade out of the churchy bits with him, as she had said, or was she just kidding him on? When it came to the crunch, she might just back out.

'I wonder what's over there?' Jarryn said, nodding toward the steep, scrub-choked sides of the mountain behind the shearers' kitchen.

'Yeah, I was wondering that yesterday', Tank answered.

'We'll get some free time later on, so we can climb it and see', Jarryn said as he turned back to the fire. 'Hope breakfast's not too much longer.' Tank grinned and nodded.

The fire was just beginning to crackle into the extra wood that Jarryn had dropped onto it, when Mrs Woods rang the bell to announce breakfast. People poured from their rooms, from the showers, from wherever they were, and made eagerly for the dining room.

The trestle tables were set with varying assortments of cutlery and crockery, eggs and bacon, Weetbix and porridge, toast and muesli, and all were ready for serving. Tea, coffee and Milo waited on a side cupboard with mugs and cups, teaspoons, and an enormous kettle which puffed vapour like Mum's steam iron at home; the whole room smelt delicious!

The organised chaos continued happily for several minutes until just about everyone was there; then Steven said a prayer of thanks, and people began to pile up their plates. Gemma, already seated just across from Jarryn, explained that Scarlet was still in the shower.

'Well, she's actually out of the shower now, but she wants to use her hair drier while the generator's still running', she said with a grin. Jarryn rolled his eyes and grinned in return.

Breakfast was nearly over when Scarlet finally turned up. Grabbing a plate, two pieces of toast, and a Milo, she hurriedly sat down with a sigh and surveyed everyone in her immediate surroundings.

This morning she had braided her hair back into a thick plait, and her curly fringe bounced at being left free. She wore the most outrageous colours, looking more like something from an advertisement for paint than someone on an outback camp.

'G'day, all', she smiled as she sat down and bit into her toast. 'Gosh, they get up early on these camps, don't they?'

'Well, there's lots to do, you see', Gemma responded. 'If we slept in, we'd miss half of it.'

A sudden quirky grin lifted one corner of Scarlet's mouth as she swallowed her toast, and she looked straight at Tank. She didn't say anything, though, and Jarryn pointed out that part of what they *did* have to do that morning was to clean the toilets and mop out the showers. Gemma screwed up her nose. Scarlet crossed her eyes, and Tank slid down into his chair, but while outwardly he groaned, inwardly he was singing.

Although they didn't actually organise or even mention it at all, Scarlet and Tank slipped away quietly just as all the others, carrying Bibles, notebooks, and pencils, were filing into the lounge. They had almost acted on impulse, catching each other's eye at the last moment and gesturing a let's-get-out-of-here movement with the head.

'I'd better leave a note, I guess', Tank said as they dodged out of sight of the last few people moving into the meeting room. Scarlet looked surprised. 'Why?' she asked.

'Jarryn'll wonder where I've gone', Tank explained.

'Well, I haven't told Gemma', Scarlet reasoned. 'She'd only try and stop me if I did. As it is, this will probably cause a bit of a stir, but she'll get over it.'

Tank looked hard at Scarlet for a moment, trying to gauge how serious she was. She looked straight back, green eyes huge and sparkling. 'It won't take long', he said finally, and ran to the room he shared with Jarryn.

Quickly he scribbled a note: 'Gone for a walk over the big one with Scarlet. Back by lunchtime. T.', and left it on the bed under Jarryn's torch. Scarlet, who had followed, waited by the door.

'They won't even miss us', she said.

'Jarryn will', Tank replied firmly, and this time Scarlet looked hard at him.

'Come on, let's go', he said.

'Where?'

'Up the mountain.'

'Which one?'

'The one behind the kitchen. It's the biggest one I've seen around here, so the view should be pretty speccy.'

They set off, carefully avoiding the kitchen in case Mrs Paige or Mrs Woods saw them, and were soon on the lower slopes of the mountain's base.

As mountains go, the Gawler Ranges were not all that huge, but they *were* mountains, and steep, forbidding, rocky, scrubby, and exhausting at that. This climb made the jaunt of the night before feel like a gentle lap around the footy oval. Here thick scrub scratched their arms and faces, branches barred their way like arms trying to hold them back, steep, steep shoulders and folds in the landscape made their legs tremble with effort. Sections of sheer granite rock face sent them way out from their original course in order to go higher, and loose scree, gravel, and rocks moved underfoot, hurtling backwards and downwards and threatening to take them too on a crazy, uncontrolled slippery dip that would certainly end painfully.

Although the day was still, yet cool from the early morning frost, both Scarlet and Tank had already removed their jumpers and tied them around their waists. Sweat beaded, joined other beads on their foreheads and necks, and ran in rivulets down their backs and off their chins. Both were red-faced with the effort they were putting into the climb, and neither had any thought of giving up.

Several times they stopped to get their breath, choosing, wherever they could, a more open spot to allow the cool air and any breeze there might be to reach them. There was no breath left for conversation, so they just sat until one or other of them got up and set off again.

From time to time they could hear a quick thump-thump as a startled kangaroo barged off through the scrub, birds twittering further ahead suddenly fell into silence as they approached, and once, way overhead, a pair of eagles circled lazily. The scrub did not lessen as they neared the summit. In fact, it was difficult to tell when they had actually reached the top, except that suddenly they were not climbing any more.

There was no view from where they stood, however, just thick scrub and rocks, so after

27

another brief rest Tank set off again, through the scrub and directly across the top. After a short walk he came upon a clearer spot, and from there such a fabulous view rolled away before them that they just stood there and looked for a full two minutes.

They were on the crest of the mountain, looking down into a great gully that slashed across their view like a red line through a misspelt word. Opposite, on the far side of the gully, mountains creased and folded with what must have been dozens of waterfalls and creeks, to feed an enormous watercourse far, far below. Then, up and over, beyond the opposite mountains, more and more scrub-clad peaks purpled away into the distance, where they just seemed to mist out against the blue sky. It was one of the wildest, most beautiful sights Tank had ever seen in his life.

'It's unbelievable!' Scarlet sighed.

'Sure is', Tank agreed.

'I don't regret one scratch now, after seeing this.'

Tank grinned.

'Shall we go down?' Scarlet asked.

Tank looked at his watch. it had taken over an hour to climb the mountain, but it was still quite early. 'Maybe, if we just go to the watercourse at the bottom and have a look, but don't go any further. We should be able to get back to camp and still have time up our sleeves.'

Scarlet nodded agreement, and very carefully they began to work their way down.

It was, in a different way, just as difficult going down as coming up. The steepness seemed to suck them downwards, making them grab at trees, rocks, and even grass on occasions to stop any sort of momentum building up. Some of the grasses were rigid and sharp, spearing through their sneakers, socks, and jeans, prodding them painfully in the ankles and legs. Others were soft and lay down underfoot, creating a smooth slippery surface which their shoes could find no grip on at all. Added to that were the insurmountable piles of red granite that suddenly crossed their path and the miniature cliffs that dropped away below them, so it soon became apparent that going down was not going to be any easier at all.

'I thing we're onto the very beginning of a waterfall here!' Tank exclaimed after a short while.

'Why?' Scarlet wanted to know.

'Look, all these rocks in this depression here, there's nothing growing between them, and there's black stuff down the middle of them, like you see on the waterfalls when they're dry. When it rains, that stuff gets real slimy and slippery.'

Carefully they clambered over the boulders, down and down, until suddenly it all opened out. They were on a wide granite promontory about a quarter way down the mountain and overlooking a magnificent view of the big watercourse at the bottom. And right underfoot they discovered the sheerest, smoothest, deadliest looking little cliff face they had yet come across. It dropped some thirty metres to a pile of boulders below, and there wasn't a ledge or crack or anything else to be seen the whole way down.

'Wow!' Tank sighed. ''What a place to hang glide from!'

Gemma and Jarryn had realised almost at the same time that Tank and Scarlet were

missing, but as they were already seated and the first session had begun, there wasn't anything they could do about it.

Jarryn felt a little betrayed that Tank would go off and not tell him. For all his talk against anything 'Christianic', as he called it, Tank often displayed thoughtfulness to a degree that would put some Christians to shame. It just wasn't like him to disappear without saying anything. Because of this, Jarryn realised, he was unable to really concentrate on what Steven was talking about. He contented himself as best he could by praying in his mind and hoping like mad that God would make it all come out right in the end.

Maybe Tank was just so wrapped up in Scarlet he wasn't thinking straight.

After the first session was finished, there was a break for a drink, something to eat, and a walk around to loosen up. Jarryn made straight for Gemma.

She looked up as he approached, spread her hands wide, and shrugged. 'I've got no idea', she answered his unspoken question. 'Scarlet didn't say anything to me this morning.'

Jarryn sat down in the empty seat next to her. 'Tank didn't say anything either', he sighed. 'I really wish . . .' He stopped himself finishing that. He'd been going to say that he really wished he hadn't invited Tank. 'He *always* tells me when he's going off some-where', he said, 'like I always tell him. It's a deal we made years ago when we first started exploring in the Landcruiser.'

Gemma looked at Jarryn. 'Maybe he's left a note . . .' she suggested.

Jarryn jerked to his feet and was across the room in no time at all, out across the gravel to their room, and was sitting on his bed reading before Gemma even realised what he'd actually gone to do.

Tank hadn't let him down after all. Taking the note, he went back to find Gemma, who was now in the kitchen helping herself to some chocolate cake.

'Well, at least we know where they've gone', she said. ''Scarlet often does this. You get used to it after a while.'

Jarryn looked at Gemma. She really was a most likeable person. He wondered if Scarlet appreciated that.

'What should we do?' she asked.

'Nothing probably', he told her. 'They said they'd be back by lunchtime. That's only about another hour-and-a-half away, so it's not worth trying to chase them up. If they're not back after lunch, we'll tell someone then.'

'That makes sense, I guess', Gemma agreed. 'We'd better get back to the lounge, or we'll miss the next session too.'

They went.

True to Tank's word, the two runaways slipped back into camp just as everyone was coming out of the lounge. Scarlet made straight for the bathroom to check her hair and wash the dirt and sweat from her face, and Tank made for his room.

Sure enough the note was gone, and Tank was suddenly glad he'd written it and not gone off without saying anything. That would have broken the agreement he and Jarryn had, and Tank didn't believe you should ever break agreements unless you had a compelling reason, like two broken legs or your mother unaccountably demanding that you clean your room *before* you do *anything* else whatsoever.

Jarryn arrived at the door just as Tank turned to go out. There was a silence for a moment. Then 'What's up there?' Jarryn asked off-handedly.

Tank gave a mental sigh of relief. 'Only the most fabulous view you've ever seen in your entire life', he replied, 'but the way up is sheer torture'.

If anyone else had noticed Scarlet and Tank's absence that morning, no-one mentioned it, and after lunch they joined the group to go abseiling as if nothing had happened at all.

Steven took them to a small rock face, tucked safely into the base of a mountain just around from the bald one they had climbed the night before. The rock face was craggy and cracked into geometric fingers and octagonal shapes standing some ten metres high. At the top he sat everyone down, and began to talk to them about safety.

'Your rope is all you have between you and a fall', he explained. 'It's vital that you check it thoroughly every time you intend to use it.' He looked around at each one in turn. 'I can't stress that to you enough', he added. 'Ropes wear quickly in this sport, and you just cannot afford to take risks.'

Carefully Steven took them through all the safety procedures, showed them how to look for wear and tear on the ropes, taught them knots, demonstrated different methods people used in abseiling, and then actually showed them what he was going to get them to do.

It looked so easy! Within minutes he was at the bottom of the cliff and getting ready to climb up again. Tank, Jarryn, and everyone else peered over the cliff edge or from the grassy shoulders on each side of it and watched. It looked great!

When Steven reached the top again, he stood grinning and looked around. 'Right', he said, 'who's first?' There was an excited murmur. 'You don't have to go down if you don't want to', he reassured them, 'but if you do, now is the time to say so.'

'I do, I'll have a go', Scarlet called out, and Steven's grin broadened. 'Somehow I had a feeling *you* would', he said, and began setting up another harness.

Chapter 4

'I told you before I even came that I wasn't keen on the holy bits', Scarlet told Gemma the next day when asked if she was going to join the Bible study. 'I don't mind some of the stuff, but it gets a bit heavy when they start preaching fire and brimstone.'

Gemma had to smile. 'He won't preach fire and brimstone . . .' she began.

'O won't he? He was warming up to it the first night we were here', Scarlet shot back.

'Well, it's true, we do have a choice, but yesterday's session was nothing like you're thinking. Anyway, you even agreed that the bit Steven said about truth was interesting.'

'It was, sort of, but I'm not ready to make a choice yet. Maybe when I'm thirty or something.'

Gemma began to say something, but gave up. It was clear that Scarlet didn't want to go to the study session, and Gemma instinctively knew that to push was the best way to drive Scarlet away altogether. It had been a miracle her coming at all, and it wouldn't do to undermine that. But, Gemma thought, what was the point of Scarlet being here at all if she didn't hear anything helpful? She sighed. 'What are you going to do then?' she asked.

'Tank and I will go back to where we were yesterday and go on from there down to the creek at the bottom. Why don't you come too, Gem? It's fabulous up there.'

'I don't think I could keep up for one thing', Gemma grinned, 'but I want to go to the studies anyway', she added.

Shrugging, Scarlet finished plaiting her hair and looped a scrunchie around the end to hold it. 'OK', she said. 'You do your thing, I'll do mine.' Gemma looked a little lost at that, and Scarlet had a sudden, unusual rush of sympathy for her. She sat down on the bed and gave her a quick hug. 'Hey, it's OK. It's only for the morning — we'll be back by lunchtime, just like yesterday, I promise.'

Gemma smiled. Scarlet could sell sand to the Arabs if she tried, Gemma decided. 'Well, be careful. Don't go getting lost or anything', she said.

Scarlet rolled her eyes. 'Gemma, you're getting worse than my mother!'

Jarryn was being very careful to stay neutral with Tank. He didn't want to tip the fine balance between the possibility of Tank joining in on some things and maybe learning something, and the possibility of turning him off so completely that he wouldn't join in anything. So it was with very carefully chosen words and tone of voice that he asked Tank what he was going to do that morning.

Tank knew it was coming and was being equally careful, but Jarryn wasn't prepared for the way Tank delivered his answer. Never, through their differences over Jarryn being a Christian, had Tank looked at him while he was speaking about it. He just never did. Now, however, he sat down on the bed opposite Jarryn, facing him and looking at him squarely.

'I don't really want to go to the study', Tank said honestly. 'Some of the things make me feel . . .' he broke off, searching for a way to put it — 'embarrassed', he said. It was the only word he could find that came close to fitting, and he knew that it would probably make Jarryn feel awful. But he had absorbed something of what Steven had said the previous night, and found that he agreed with it. Truth was a good thing, and it just happened that one of the things he'd always liked about Jarryn was his honesty. He also knew that by being honest from the beginning he could save himself a lot of trouble in the long run.

Jarryn was silent for a while. He had never known Tank to be as direct as this, and while he didn't like the reason and didn't like the idea that Tank was going off bush again, he found that he really did appreciate what Tank had just done. 'OK', he said. 'When will you be back?'

'Lunchtime again, same as yesterday.'

'Is Scarlet going too?'

'As far as I know, if Gemma doesn't talk her out of it', Tank grinned.

Jarryn grinned back. 'I don't think you've got any worries', he said.

Tank had done some planning the previous night. The day's abseiling had been a marvellous experience and something he was very keen to try again. The intense feeling that had gripped his stomach as he'd walked backwards over the edge of that cliff was something he had never felt before. Even in his most frightened moments, and he and Jarryn had shared a few of those, he had never felt anything like that. It was fear and exhilaration and horror and desire and sickness and shock and love all at the same time. It was incredible, and he wanted to do it again.

So this time he carried a backpack. In it he had put some water, food, a pair of binoculars, and the longest rope that he could find in the Landcruiser. It was a new one and was kept there in case they needed to tow anything out of a boggy patch back on the farm. Just the thing, Tank decided, for abseiling.

The day had begun much like the previous one, icy cold but with a clear blue sky and bright sunshine. Probably it would warm up quite a lot later on.

Once again Scarlet and Tank set off up the side of the mountain, forcing their way through scrub, over rocks, up, up, up until they reached the top. Then on and over until they came to the spectacular little cliff. Here they sat down to rest.

Tank took out the water bottle and offered it to Scarlet, who took it gratefully.

'Good idea, that', she said as she passed it back. 'What else have you got in there?'

'Something to eat, some binoculars, some rope . . .' he said offhandedly.

'Rope? What do you want rope for?'

Tank grinned. 'I thought it would be good to try abseiling down here.'

Scarlet looked at him, looked at the cliff, pulled the backpack toward her, and looked at the rope. 'Is it safe?' she asked.

'Yes, it's new', Tank replied, 'but I'll check it properly first, just to make sure'.

Scarlet was beaming. 'It was good fun yesterday, wasn't it?' she said.

Tank nodded. 'If we tie it around us tightly into a sort of harness, it should do the same job. There's loads of rope, and we can anchor it to that tree stump over there.'

Scarlet's eyebrows had risen a little in surprise but she didn't seem at all frightened, and Tank couldn't help but feel a rush of appreciation for the beautiful, tough, adventuresome person she was. To his way of thinking, she was perfect.

Thinking about it, planning it, now even talking about it were all exciting but easy things to do. Now, however, up here, on top of the cliff, on their own, Tank found that he was beginning to feel apprehensive. Suddenly the cliff wasn't so small, the rope didn't look *quite* thick enough, and the thought of physically stepping back off the top without having seen someone demonstrate it — not on *this* cliff, anyway — was rather awesome. But there was Scarlet busily pulling the rope out of the backpack, humming to herself, ready to try this and obviously not the least bit worried. Tank could not, for the life of him, back out now. He would be too ashamed.

Poking around in the coils of rope, he found the end and began to check along its length for signs of wear and tear. Of course there were none. He'd known that there wouldn't be; they'd only used the rope once, to tie the fridge into the ute with when they took it into town for repairs. Barely five metres at one end had been used to hold the unit steady, but it hadn't been necessary, for the fridge was already strapped in with woven straps and, as an added stabiliser, barricaded too with several bags of oats. It hadn't moved the whole trip.

But he checked anyway, just in case. Just in case there was a chance the rope was flawed and Tank could call the whole thing off without losing face. But it wasn't and he couldn't, so with a secret sigh he got up and moved toward the dead tree stump to secure the rope.

'How will you tie it to yourself?' Scarlet wanted to know.

'Just trial and error, I guess.'

He began by taking one of the two ends and looping it around his waist. Then he wrapped the rope around one thigh, then the other, and brought it back to tie again at his waist. For a moment then he didn't know what else to do.

'Take it over your shoulders', Scarlet suggested. 'That way you shouldn't flip over and fall out headfirst to the bottom.'

Tank didn't like the image that sprang to mind at this, but he didn't reply, and he quickly set about crossing the rope over his shoulder, through the loop at his waist, back over the shoulder, and then tied again tightly at the middle of his chest. If he lost his grip now, he thought wryly, he'd just hang like a netful of cargo over the hold of a ship — but he wouldn't fall out!

Carefully he tested everything for comfort and safety, checked the tree stump to see if it would support his weight, picked up the other end of the rope and, swallowing air in a suddenly desert-dry mouth, he moved toward the edge of the cliff.

Although Jarryn went along to the study feeling quite OK about Tank and what he was doing, he found during the course of the morning that he wasn't concentrating at all. His mind kept wandering off over the mountain to where he knew Tank and Scarlet would be exploring. Tank had been really enthusiastic as he had described the little cliff, the great gully, and the mountains beyond, and Jarryn had been caught up with that enthusiasm to a point where he now wanted to go and see it for himself.

At the start he forced himself to concentrate on what Steven was saying, but more and more often he found that his mind drifted, his eyes locked unseeing onto the floor, and his desire to see the other side of the mountain grew steadily by the minute. By the morning break he had lost all track of what Steven was talking about, and had more or less decided that there really wasn't any point in being there anyway if he couldn't concentrate. He grabbed a huge slab of cake and a cup of Milo, and then went to find Gemma.

'I'm thinking about going over the mountain after Tank', he said simply. 'Do you want to come?'

Gemma looked at him for a moment and then looked down, thinking. 'What about the study?' she asked.

Jarryn looked uncomfortable. 'I know, but I just can't seem to concentrate', he admitted. 'I keep thinking about all the things that Tank told me. I can't remember half of what Steven's said this morning.'

Gemma nodded agreement. 'I know what you mean. I haven't been concentrating either', she said, 'but I don't think I'll go. I'd hold you up for one thing, and anyway we can't be sure we'd even find them.'

Jarryn could see sense in this, and he was also feeling guilty. He was torn between what he *felt* like doing and what he thought he *should* do, and at the back of his mind he thought he would be letting God down if he didn't stay.

He finished his slab of cake and wandered back toward their sleeping hut, still battling with his desire to follow Tank and Scarlet instead of doing what he felt he should do —

stay at the camp and go to the study. The two were so evenly balanced in his mind: responsibility and selfish want. He just couldn't choose which to follow. And what was more, he couldn't bring himself to pray about it either! The main reason was that he thought he already knew what the answer was, and if he knew the answer then the question didn't really need asking. Of course God would want him to stay at the study; surely there was no doubt about that? So why was he being so tormented with this urge to follow Tank?

Jarryn didn't know. He leant over the back of the Landcruiser and sighed. It was nearly time to go back in. Only another hour and a half and Tank and Scarlet would be back, he told himself. If he went now he would probably meet them as they returned. Stay at the study, he told himself, and he had just about made up his mind to do that when he noticed that the rope was gone.

To begin with, it didn't have any impact on Jarryn, until he remembered Tank telling him about the magnificent little cliff face he had discovered and how perfect it would be for hang-gliding from, or abseiling . . .

Surely Tank wouldn't try that? Jarryn thought, and answered himself: Yes, he probably would, especially if Scarlet was there. In fact, Scarlet was just crazy enough to have a go too!

People were beginning to move back toward the lounge, but Jarryn had already made his decision. Gemma quickly came to mind, but after a moment's hesitation he chose not to go and get her. To begin with, she hadn't sounded very keen when he had asked her earlier, and on top of that, through no fault of her own, she *would* hold him up, and suddenly Jarryn wanted to go as fast as he could. Gemma would know that he had gone. The decision made, Jarryn wasted no more time. Slipping around the side of the kitchen he set off as quickly as he could, through the scrub and onto the side of the mountain, trying all the time to remember everything Tank had mentioned that might help him to find the cliff.

Tank had tied the middle of the rope around the tree stump and left the two ends free to be used for abseiling. One end he had tied around himself to ensure that he couldn't fall too far, and the other end he used to support his weight as he worked his way backwards down the cliff. It wasn't the right way, it wasn't the way that Steven had shown them, but it was the best he could do with what they had. And it seemed to be working very well. Even though the rope was a long one, it wasn't nearly long enough to reach the bottom of the cliff, especially since they were only effectively using half its length. At best it took him down about a third of the way. It was decidedly uncomfortable at times where the rope dug under his armpits and squeezed his thighs, but it was worth it.

Now that he had taken that first step backwards off the cliff — and he had really had to *force* himself to do that — and worked his way carefully down to the full limit of the rope, he felt incredibly triumphant. He had mastered his own fear, overcome the sick feelings in his stomach, and *won*! It was a top feeling, a most amazing feeling; he felt great, sort of tough and brave and cool all at once. To celebrate, he had pushed himself outwards with his legs and swung away from the cliff in a short semicircle,

around and back again, arms and legs stretched to clumsily break the crash as he returned to the craggy granite wall.

'Hurry up!' Scarlet called down. 'You're hogging all the fun.'

'It's fantastic!' Tank called back.

'I can see that.'

'OK, I'll come up. Hang on.'

It was much harder getting back up than it had been going down. The granite had very few handholds or footrests, and often Tank had only the rope and his own strength to rely on. When he had thought of abseiling down the cliff, he hadn't really considered how he was going to get up again. With Steven, they had just unhooked themselves at the bottom and climbed back up on the less steep flanks of the abseiling spot.

Eventually he reached the top, and when he scrambled breathlessly up over the edge, his grin was so wide that Scarlet thought he must have remembered a funny joke.

'What's so funny?' she asked.

'Nothing', he answered broadly. 'It's just so great down there.'

'Well, let me have a turn then', Scarlet demanded.

Tank began to undo knots. They had pulled tight supporting his weight, and it took a little while to loosen some of them. While he was doing this, Scarlet began to loop the other free end of the rope around herself in a similar fashion, tying it around her legs, arms, and waist, ready to go the moment Tank was all undone.

Finally, she was ready. She looked at Tank, who was grinning back at her. 'It's great', he said. 'It's only scary for the first few minutes.

When you reach the end of the rope, just swing about a bit — it gives you an unreal feeling.'

Still Scarlet hesitated, though she was smiling broadly. 'Not scared are you?' Tank stirred.

'Of course not!' Scarlet bit back quickly. 'I'm just . . . mentally preparing myself.'

Tank gave a hoot of laughter which sounded very much to Scarlet as if he didn't believe her. It was true, though; she was scared, but there was no way she would ever let Tank know that. Carefully she began to work her way over the edge of the cliff and downwards.

Once she was over the edge, it wasn't so bad. Scarlet felt quite secure facing the solid red-black granite wall in front of her. She was comforted too by the fact that she didn't weigh nearly as much as Tank, and the rope had supported him easily. So for the first part of the venture everything went smoothly. Looking up, Scarlet could see Tank, lying on his stomach as she had done, peering over the top of the drop, watching her. The rope had tightened around her arms and legs, pinching her clothes and some skin too, making her squirm quickly to release it. There was a soft breeze carrying a heavy honey smell from the nearby scrub, and the sun was warm on her back.

When she reached the rope's limit, she allowed herself to release her weight into the makeshift harness she had tied herself into and relaxed her hold on the loose end. Looking down was her first mistake.

Between her feet the view slid down a rock face like a fall of liquid granite that suddenly hardened. It fell away, down, and exploded into hundreds of static boulders, stone droplets, round, smooth, and undoubtably *hard* .

Scarlet's gaze continued around then, until she looked out behind her. Another mistake!

Far, far below, the great gully gaped upwards; far, far behind, the opposite mountains rose to watch. On either side of her there was nothing. Just nothing! She felt that if she leant back she would flip over, and if she reached sideways what was there to grab? In fact, now she came to think of it, how was she to get back up again? In front of her the granite cliff rose smooth, flat, and shapeless.

Real fear, far more urgent than the excited fear she had felt earlier, now twisted inside her. It sent shivers of apprehension rippling outwards, down her arms and legs in repeated waves. Her hair crept around on her scalp, and beads of sweat that had nothing at all to do with being hot burst out all over her body, her face, her hands, everywhere. Hardly daring to move in case everything that held her there should suddenly fail, she fought the rising panic and began to look for handholds, footholds, any tiny little thing at all on the cliff face that could offer her an anchor, a safe hold to grab at and hang on to.

'Tank?' she called softly, not daring to speak too loud for fear of she didn't know what.

'What?' came the comfortable answer. It was OK for him, he was on top!

'H . . . how did you get up again?'

'Climbed, of course. There's not much to hold on to, is there?'

Scarlet closed her eyes for a moment. She was beginning to feel sick, but having her eyes closed made her head spin, and that was a sensation she could well do without.

'Why didn't you tell me?' she accused, her fear coming through sharply, like anger.

Tank was taken aback. 'I don't know. Just didn't think, I guess. Why, what's wrong?'

'I'm stuck, Tank. I can't get back up.' Suddenly with this admission the panic rose up inside like a huge black shadow. 'I can't reach as far as you. I can't get back up. I'm stuck! You should have told me. You should have known . . .' The shadow was seeping in fast, filling her head, filling her heart, filling everything until she was screaming. Screaming and sobbing and hanging there, helplessly, hopelessly, in the soft honey fragrance of the mallee trees and the warm gentle sunshine. The shadow swamped her and blotted it all out then, everything, in an enormous wave of hysteria.

Chapter 5

The mountain was more rugged, far steeper, and much more difficult to climb than Jarryn had expected. Several times he had to change direction and find an easier path because the most direct way suddenly became impossible; and he found that he had to stop and catch his breath more and more often — it was just so *steep*.

For some reason, however, Jarryn felt compelled to keep going. He didn't know which direction Tank and Scarlet had taken, but he guessed he might get a better idea from the top. Tank had said something about a clearing part-way down the other side, bearing right, so Jarryn's first goal was to reach the top, and then try to find that clearing.

The summit was not immediately evident, so Jarryn was not really sure when he reached it, but it seemed that the ground levelled out a bit, rounded off at a much less steep angle, and he soon realised that he wasn't climbing any more. There was not much to see, however. All around him was thick scrub, mallee, wattles, and gums. Where, he wondered, was this fabulous view?

Carefully choosing a direction which bore to the right, Jarryn continued. He would have loved a drink, but it hadn't occurred to him that the climb would be this difficult, or that he would get so hot and thirsty. Once he thought he heard voices and nearly called out, but when five or six nanny-goats, kids in tow, charged away into the scrub some moments later, Jarryn amended the idea and stopped listening. When he heard someone begin to scream, however, he stopped in his tracks and listened very hard. It sounded like Scarlet.

There was no doubt about it; the sound was somewhere back to his left and below, down the mountain side. Jarryn couldn't make out any words because there were echoes reverberating back from the surrounding mountains and mixing, five or six syllables later, distorting it. But one thing was very clear: Scarlet was just about hysterical!

Tank was horrified. To begin with, he thought that Scarlet was stirring him with a fake telling-off. Then he accepted that she might perhaps be a little angry with him for not mentioning how difficult it was; and it had been difficult, even for him, to climb back up again. But when he realised that Scarlet was scared, really scared, he was so lost for words that he didn't know what to say, so he said nothing and watched helplessly while she gave in to hysterics and panicked in a big way. For maybe a full minute and a half, she sobbed and screamed and swore and blamed, but then, suddenly, she fell frighteningly silent.

Even as he watched, she seemed to go limp, release her hold on the cliff face, and very gently, like slow motion on video, float outwards to dangle like a lightly weighted plumbline, softly following circular paths in the air. With real alarm now, Tank realised that she must have fainted.

The silence was as bad as Scarlet's noise had been moments before, and strangely, Tank felt very uncomfortable about breaking it.

Distractedly he got to his feet, looked down at the limp figure slowly swaying on the rope below, and then looked helplessly about him, at the scrub, the opposite mountains, the sky, anything. He wondered frantically what he should do. Could he pull her up? He didn't think so, not on his own. He couldn't reach her from either side of the cliff face, and he couldn't climb down to her, or up from the bottom, without another rope.

Maybe he should go for help! He wanted to dismiss that idea the moment he thought of it because it would mean all sorts of trouble. After all, they'd just gone out and tried almost exactly the sort of dumb, stupid, foolhardy prank that Steven had warned them against the day before. There was definitely going to be big trouble if this episode got out.

But if he couldn't get Scarlet back to the top without help, then obviously they were going to be late back and Jarryn would be sure to get people together to come and look for them. If only Jarryn was here *now*! Tank thought.

He looked over the cliff again. Scarlet still hadn't moved. She was flopping forward onto the rope which supported her weight, her arms hanging loosely, slightly forward away from her body, her legs sort of turned inwards, pigeon-toed in a way, which made her seem terribly helpless.

'Scarlet?' he whispered, although he didn't know why he whispered. There was no answer. He tried again, louder this time. Still no reply. What on earth was he to do? What would Jarryn do if he was here?

Tank sighed and curled his lips at this in a wry sort of grimace. Pray probably, he answered himself, and sat down again. Still, he found himself acknowledging, things would feel a whole lot better if Jarryn *was* here.

'G'day', Jarryn said, as he pushed his way through from between two wattles and joined Tank.

Tank jumped at the sound of Jarryn's voice, and quickly, guiltily he peered into the scrub behind to see if anyone else was with him.

'Man, am I glad to see you! Is anyone with you?'

'No. Where's Scarlet?'

'Down there', Tank said, pointing over the cliff and looking rather ashamed of himself.

Jarryn looked at Tank and went to peer over the edge. Tank joined him. Scarlet was moving. She lifted her hands to grab the rope supporting her, looked tentatively upwards, and groaned.

'What happened?' Jarryn asked Tank, and Tank told him.

There was a long silence after Tank finished telling him what had happened. Jarryn's first thought was to head back to camp and get help, but that would mean heaps of unpleasantness from the organisers, and they'd probably all get sent home early. That would then mean heaps more unpleasantness from their parents.

'She's awake', Tank said, sliding back from the edge of the cliff to sit up beside Jarryn. 'I sure hope she doesn't panic again.'

Jarryn dropped to his stomach and slithered forward to look down at Scarlet. 'Hey!' he called. Scarlet looked up. Her face looked white and scared, her eyes were like huge dark blots. 'How're you going?' he joked softly.

'Pull me up, Jarryn, please. I'm *terrified*!' She was fighting hard not to cry, and Jarryn was grateful for that; he hated it when girls cried.

'We'll try. Just hang in there a bit longer, OK?'

'Not the best choice of words . . .' Tank remarked as Jarryn stood up. Jarryn couldn't help but smile. He hadn't thought about what he was saying; he'd just wanted to be reassuring.

'What do we do?' Tank asked.

Jarryn's face straightened, and he sighed. 'There's only one thing I can think of that *might* work. I saw it on the Leyland Brothers on TV once. They were pulling a Landcruiser out of a boggy patch without another car. But it's pretty slow, and the first part's going to be really hard.'

'Why?'

'We have to tie a loop in the rope that's holding Scarlet, and who knows what effect that could have!'

Tank pulled his hand distractedly through his hair and blew a sibilant whistle. 'I'd better ask her', he said after a moment.

Jarryn watched as Tank got down onto his stomach and wormed his way to the cliff's edge, and then he set off to look for a couple of really strong branches.

Tank wasn't sure how Scarlet would react when he spoke to her. After all, it was his fault she was down there and couldn't get up again. She might not even answer him.

'Scarlet?' he called carefully. She looked up but didn't say anything. 'We're going to try and pull you up somehow . . .' he began. This was really difficult. '. . . We have to tie a loop in the rope somehow before we can start . . .'

'It's OK. I'll be all right as long as I don't look down or behind. I promise not to yell or anything again . . . Just get me out of this, please.'

She was still fighting back tears, but she wasn't mad with him! Tank felt relief ease his chest. 'Good on you', he said, and turned back to see what Jarryn was working on.

'First we've got to tie a loop in the rope', Jarryn explained. 'Then we have to use these two branches to make a sort of winder.'

'A what?'

'Look, we stand one of these here . . .' Tank watched as Jarryn stood a stripped tree branch upright on the ground. 'When the rope has a loop in it we put this one through the loop', he indicated the second branch, 'and cross it at right angles against the one standing up. Then one of us walks round and round pushing the horizontal branch, turning it all around. It *should* start to wind the rope around the upright one and bring Scarlet up at the same time.'

Tank was impressed. It was a brilliant idea, and he looked at Jarryn with undisguised admiration. 'Where do you get all these ideas?' he asked.

Jarryn screwed up his face. 'I just make them up for fun', he joked. 'Anyway, I don't know if it'll work yet.'

Tank couldn't see any way that it wouldn't work. Once explained, it seemed so simple.

'The hardest part is going to be tying the loop. How long do you think you can hold Scarlet's weight for?'

Tank's eyebrows rose and his face blanked. He shrugged. 'I don't know', he answered honestly.

'We'll just have to give it a go and find out, then. We can pull her up together, until we get enough slack in the rope to tie the loop, and then you'll have to hold her there while I make the knot.'

Tank's face grimaced. 'How fast can you tie knots?' he asked.

Jarryn grinned. 'Don't know. I've never tried to find out', he said. 'I'll go and tell Scarlet.'

Tank followed, and while Jarryn briefly explained what they were going to do, Tank took hold of the rope and began experimenting to find which was the most secure grip he could use.

'Let's hope it works', Jarryn said. 'We'll have to start from here and pull almost to where we left the branches.'

Tank eyes the distance. It was about four metres.

'Then you hold her while I tie the loop', Jarryn added. 'Simple.'

'Simple', Tank echoed.

'Let's do it.'

Tank grabbed the rope nearest the cliff edge, and Jarryn chose his place half way between Tank and where they'd left the branches. It wasn't just Scarlet's weight that made it difficult; it was also the drag of the rope as it grated over the granite edge, the quick slip of coarse fibre scorching in their hands and squeezing their flesh where they had looped it for better grip, and the sudden lack of footholds, cracks, stable rocks, anything which would give their feet purchase so that they could brace themselves against the slide of fine gravel on smooth granite. And for Tank, the abominable length of time it took to reach their goal was only the beginning. He hadn't realised how much weight his friend was taking until Jarryn eased up, carefully, to let Tank take over. Quickly Tank had to adjust his grip, shift his weight, and find an even better purchase for his feet. Even then he was not really holding.

Very slowly he could feel that he was being pulled back. He was facing away from Jarryn, so he couldn't see how Jarryn was going tying the knot. Tank's face screwed up with effort, sweat poured down his back, and he found he was holding his breath to prevent himself from letting go. He *mustn't* do that! He imagined seeing Scarlet's body drop and jerk to a sudden halt as it reached the rope's limit — a horrible idea, but it renewed his resolution not to give in until he felt Jarryn take up some of the weight again.

'We can let it back down now. I've tied the loop.' It took an awesome amount of will power to let go slowly, and when he finally eased his hands from around the rope Tank found he was trembling quite violently.

Jarryn went to the cliff's edge and looked down at Scarlet. She was spinning very slowly, like an unwound yoyo, and she had covered her face with both hands. 'We've tied the loop', he told her. 'It won't take long now.' Scarlet didn't answer.

Tank had one branch upright on the ground and the other one through the loop, positioned and ready for action when Jarryn got back. 'Have I got this right?' he asked.

Jarryn looked. 'Yep, start turning.'

Tank began to walk. The rope grabbed the upright branch as if it was magnetised, and suddenly Tank found he had to push, hard, to force the horizontal branch around, but it was nowhere near the struggle it had been earlier. Round and round and round he went, the upright branch in one hand while the other branch, braced against his thighs and held steady with his other hand, forced the rope to wind.

57

It was working! The rope dragged painfully over the granite cliff's edge, powdering as it did so, like smoke in twigs just before it bursts into flame. Jarryn returned to the cliff to help Scarlet as soon as she reached the top. He hoped she wouldn't panic again when she had to scramble up over the edge.Gradually Scarlet was hoisted to the rim. Jarryn saw that she continued to cover her face with her hands, but between her fingers, as she came closer, he noticed the pallor of her skin, a horrible grey-white colour.

As her head came up level, Jarryn reached out and grabbed her arms. 'You've got to climb over here now', he said. 'It's the last bit, then you're safe.'

Scarlet dropped her hands from her face and immediately grabbed for Jarryn's arms. Like a drowning rat at passing driftwood, Scarlet scrabbled over the edge, climbed unsteadily to her feet, and hobbled as quickly as she could away from the edge of the cliff. When she felt she was far enough away, she half fell, half sat down, and burst into tears.

Horrified, Jarryn and Tank looked at each other. They had no idea what to do when girls cried. Uncomfortably they both busied themselves unwinding the rope from the branches, and hoped like mad that she'd get over it quickly.

Scarlet did. Within a minute she was standing up and quietly untying herself. Still very pale, she walked over to Jarryn and Tank with her end of the rope. 'I think we should be getting back', she said quietly, 'or people will start to wonder where we are', and then she began to walk away. 'Thanks for . . . getting me out of that', she said, and then she was gone.

Chapter 6

Jarryn and Tank took a little longer to get back to camp than Scarlet, but they knew she was there because they saw her cover the last twenty metres to her sleeping hut at a run just as they broke free of the lower scrub.

Lunch was in progress, and both Jarryn and Tank discovered that they were starving. There was no sign of Gemma.

The afternoon schedule involved a goat hunt. This meant a quick trip in cars along the dirt road to some nearby plains where Andrew had spotted goats the day before, and then some mountain climbing to catch them. Jarryn and Tank hadn't said much on the way down the mountain; they had both been too wrapped in their own thoughts. But now they looked at each other and agreed that a goat hunt was an excellent idea.

'I wonder if Scarlet will go?' Tank said aloud.

'Dunno. She didn't look too bright though, did she? I wouldn't mind betting she doesn't go', Jarryn replied.

'What about Gemma?' Tank asked.

Jarryn shrugged. 'I haven't seen here. She's probably with Scarlet.'

'Should we go and see how she is?' Tank asked.

'If you want to', Jarryn said.

Tank thought about it for a moment, and then made up his mind. 'No, I reckon we'll go and chase goats and catch up with her later. She might be feeling better by then.'

This seemed by far the best idea to Jarryn, who agreed readily. 'I'll go and put some fuel in

59

the Landcruiser', he said.

'I'm going to get some more to eat', replied Tank.

Mrs Paige was the first to see the herd, half way up the lower slopes of a mountain, between shrubs and bushes and around rocks. They were all colours, all shapes, all sizes. It was an enormous herd; there must have been nearly a hundred goats, Jarryn guessed, and as the convoy of utes, cars, four-wheel drives and Landcruisers rumbled to a halt at the bottom, they all took off — upwards.

Straight away people were pouring out of their vehicles after them. Doors were left wide open, jumpers dangled off bushes as people took them off on the run, and bleats, baas, and raucous wails mixed with squeals of delight, excited instructions, and howls of both triumph and despair as they either caught or missed their goat.

Goats of every colour streamed everywhere. Nannies called to kids, which bleated a reply, and, way ahead, three billygoats charged upwards in different directions toward the top of the mountain, leading three follow-the-leader lines of trailing goats behind them. Fawn and black, black and white, deep brown, mottled, patched, and some strikingly symmetrical in markings, the goats dodged, leapt, swerved, and raced to get away from this horrible mob of people.

Once a goat was caught, it had to be brought back to a central place near the cars, where everyone swapped details of their catch and took photos. Then the goats were released to follow, suspiciously and dazedly, the now disappearing herd over the top of the mountain.

Now and then the goats' flight alarmed a mob of kangaroos, and even one or two emus were flushed out by the chase. Galahs rose shrieking at the disturbance, startled lizards dissolved under rocks, and squeals of helpless laughter rolled around on the plain. It should have been great.

It *was* great, but to Tank it would have been better if he knew that Scarlet was OK. She *had* looked pretty awful. In fact, the more he thought about it, the more shocked he felt at how grey and ill she had looked.

Steadily, throughout the afternoon, he grew more quiet and withdrawn until, by the time they were on their way back, he was genuinely worried. 'You don't suppose she'll have nightmares and get all neurotic, do you?' Tank asked as they drove.

'Who? Scarlet? I don't think so. Why?'

'She . . . looked different.'

'Probably the shock. She was pretty scared', Jarryn pointed out.

Neither Gemma nor Scarlet turned up at tea that evening, and by now Tank was stewing. He felt guilty. It *was* his fault! He should have realised. He should, at least, have noticed that if he had trouble climbing back up the cliff again, then Scarlet would have even more trouble. She wasn't nearly as tall as he was. And what if the rope had broken? Or what if she had a heart condition?

Never before had Tank felt a need to apologise for something he had done. Apologising was almost like admitting you were weak, but right now he felt he *had* to go and say sorry to Scarlet. Because he was! He was sorry that his actions had caused this result, and he really did need to know if she was OK.

'I'm going around to their hut to see if I can find out what's going on', Tank announced some time after tea. 'Do you want to come?'

Jarryn thought for a moment. 'Yeah, OK.'

Tank felt relieved.

The door was closed, and even though the generator was running, there was no light on. Their knock brought no answer.

'I guess we'll have to wait till morning', Jarryn said. Tank nodded grimly, turning for their own hut. 'I think I'll go to bed anyway', he said. 'It's been a pretty busy day one way and another.'

Jarryn nodded. 'I'll be in later. They're playing Storm the Lantern round the fire tonight.' Tank nodded in return, said goodnight, and went to bed.

He couldn't sleep, though. He replayed the events of that morning over and over and over in his mind. How could he have been so stupid? he scolded himself. He had never seen himself as being stupid before. He'd always thought he had plenty of commonsense and initiative. It wasn't a very good feeling to realise that he wasn't foolproof after all. What would have happened if Jarryn hadn't come along?

And how had he come to be there, anyway? When he'd asked, Jarryn had just said that he couldn't concentrate and had decided to follow. Coincidence, that was all, but what timing!

When he thought about it, it wasn't the first time Jarryn had 'rescued' him from tricky situations. Mostly they were small things, but there were one or two big things too, like the adventure with the ostriches, where Tank had jumped in without thinking and ended up in the wrong, and Jarryn had never blamed him or stirred him about those times. Tank's insides squirmed now as he allowed thoughts of everything he could remember being wrong about to wash over him and punish him; things he'd done to the kids at school, the way he treated his parents sometimes, and Jarryn; selfish things that he did just to please himself, or just did not think about, or that he did to make himself look good to other people. But he wasn't good! He was stupid! He'd proved that to himself this morning! *He didn't want to be that way*, but it looked as if he was stuck with it. Once you'd done things, you'd done them, and there was no way you could undo them, ever again.

Jarryn didn't go to the fire straight away. He went for a walk along the dirt road that led away from the shearers' quarters instead. There was a brilliant moon up and the stars flashed like firework sparklers, but Jarryn didn't really notice them. He knew Tank well enough to recognise that he was pretty upset about what had happened that morning. Probably, if Tank had been able to see Scarlet this afternoon and talk to her, to find out if she was all right, things would have been easier, but it hadn't worked out like that.

Not knowing was the worst kind of punishment sometimes, and Jarryn had to admit that although she was physically safe, he had never, ever, seen anyone look as bad as Scarlet had looked when he had helped her up over the edge of that cliff. And Tank was pretty observant; he would have noticed too. Jarryn guessed that Tank would be feeling pretty bad right now, and that that was why he'd gone to bed early. Jarryn, however, had no idea what to do about it.

Should he try to talk to Tank? The idea froze in his mind. He couldn't. Yet weren't good friends supposed to try and help? Maybe this was his chance to talk to Tank about Jesus? The idea brought such a wave of horror and rejection with it that Jarryn was shocked at himself. Fine Christian he was being! God was handing him a perfect opportunity, and yet if it was the last thing in the world he had to do, Jarryn knew he couldn't do it. There were too many layers of differences between himself and Tank — layers to do with Jarryn becoming a Christian. They had had to agree to disagree about that and then bridge that difference in order to continue with their friendship, and it had all happened without a word being spoken. To open all that up on top of what Tank must be going through now, would not, Jarryn was quite sure, help Tank one bit.

He sighed. 'I can't do it, Lord', he said softly. 'Please don't make me. I know I've been pray-ing for him and everything, and I *should* try and tell him about you, but I just can't. Please, will *you* help him?'

There was nothing else he could do, so he turned around and headed back for the camp fire. Maybe the morning would bring some answers.

To Jarryn's and Tank's relief, Scarlet turned up for breakfast. They had just sat down to eat, when she and Gemma came in. Tank wasn't sure what to do. Sit there? Pretend nothing had happened? Stand up, go and talk? What if she threw a tantrum at him or ignored him? Jarryn didn't have the same hassles, and readily acknowledged Gemma's wave with a grin.

The girls brought their breakfast over and sat down opposite. Tank looked carefully at Scarlet, who smiled at him. The relief was as unbearable as the waiting, Tank thought to himself.

Jarryn noticed that Scarlet looked somehow different. She seemed more subdued, but beautiful at the same time. Gemma gave Jarryn a secret wink and smiled. She too seemed to be beaming from the inside, and Jarryn wanted to know what had happened.

They ate breakfast and listened while Andrew outlined the day's plans. They discovered they were on dish duty again, and kept up a cheerful front until, at last, they were free to talk more personally.

Without anything being said, Tank and Scarlet moved off toward the gate by the shearing shed, and Gemma and Jarryn sat down on the kitchen step.

Once again Tank was stuck for words. He knew all the things he wanted to say, and he had lots of questions to ask, but he couldn't, he felt, just start blurting them all out. While he wrestled with this, Scarlet too wrestled with her own problem. Finally she did what Tank couldn't.

'I . . . want to say sorry for the way I behaved yesterday', she began.

Tank looked surprised. 'You! It should be me who says sorry. It was *my* idea, and I didn't even think about you not being able to get back up again. It was the dumbest idea I've ever had!'

'I didn't have to climb down', she pointed out. Tank was silent a moment, guilt and self-dislike washing over him again.

'I did a lot of thinking yesterday', Scarlet continued. 'What happened at the cliff . . . well, it sort of pointed out to me that I might not always get out of the things I get myself into.'

Tank was lost. 'What do you mean?'

'Yesterday, before I went over the mountain, Gemma tried to tell me that we had to make a choice about our life, where we are going. I told her I didn't want to choose yet; maybe when I'm thirty was what I said.'

Tank stayed silent. Was Scarlet telling him she'd gone and become a Christian?

'Well yesterday, hanging in front of that cliff, absolutely scared witless, I faced death! I know this sounds really weak and stupid to you, but I honestly believed I was going to die. Tank, I was so scared I wet my pants.' She looked down, shame tinting her cheeks pink.

Tank looked down too, feeling uncomfortable for himself and for Scarlet too. He hadn't known that, and wished that she hadn't told him.

'Anyway', she continued, 'when I got back to camp I was in a bit of a mess. Well, a lot of a mess really, but luckily Gemma was in our hut and I just cried and cried and cried.'

Tank nodded, but still couldn't bring himself to say anything.

'It was awful. When you're really sure you're going to die, you see things . . . altogether differently. And I *knew* if I died, I was going to hell. No-one would save me! Not God, not Jesus, not the Holy Spirit — nobody — because I hadn't wanted them to. I hadn't let Jesus be Lord. And it seemed sort of too late then.'

Tank felt anger stir in the back of his mind, but he pushed it down. Scarlet sighed, shrugged, and flapped her hands against her sides. 'So last night we went round to see Mrs Woods, and she and Gemma and I prayed, and I decided to become a Christian.'

Just like that! Tank thought. All the apologies that *he* had wanted to say seemed silly now. She wasn't blaming him anyway, but somehow he still felt guilty. He still carried all that stuff he had recognised about himself with him, and if Scarlet had ranted and raved and made him suffer he would have borne it gladly. And then, after she had finally forgiven him, *if* she had forgiven him, he would have been free! But this way, the guilt was still his. He stared at a point far away in the distance. There was nothing there but a bit of bluebush among a whole plain full of bluebushes. If he moved his eyes he knew he would never really be sure he could find that same bush again.

Scarlet watched him. She didn't know what he was thinking, or feeling. Maybe he was angry because, after all she'd said before about not wanting to be a Christian, here she was telling him that she'd changed her mind.

'It's good, you know, being a Christian. It's not what you think', she said.

Tank looked down at her and nodded. 'We'd better get back to the others', was all he said.

Chapter 7

Tank and Scarlet both went to the morning study. Scarlet wanted to. Tank did not, but he thought it might look as if he was sulking if he sat in his sleeping hut all morning. Quietly he stared at nothing in particular, intending not to listen, not to participate, and not to show the least bit of interest. From time to time he did look across to Scarlet, who now seemed to be soaking up Steven's words like a dry sponge soaking up water. His stomach twisted inside him.

The afternoon's activity was a trip to a place called Stone Dam, a drive of about three-quarters of an hour, so immediately after lunch they all set about checking the oil, water, and fuel in their cars.

They set off, following the convoy of other cars, along the red grit track which had brought them to the camp and which continued on past the shearing shed in a northerly direction. It wound between the mountains, twisting and turning, sometimes corrugated, sometimes with washed-out hollows and ditches where the wheel tracks sank dangerously low and the ridge in between rose dangerously high. On either side of the road the mountains shouldered each other, as if for a better look. From time to time the convoy would come out onto a plain, flat and wide. Here little mobs of startled sheep would look up in alarm and lumber clumsily away through the sparse shrubbery to huddle in bigger mobs from a safer distance and watch. Wedge-tailed eagles were common, and often a road-runner lizard would skim across in front of them, only just in time to escape being squashed.

Flat plains alternated with heavy scrub and encroaching mountain sides, and occasionally they had to negotiate a dry creek bed. The early morning cold had given way to a good midday heat, and Jarryn hoped that this Stone Dam place had some water in it so that he could go for a swim.

Tank hadn't said much since his talk with Scarlet, and Jarryn didn't want to seem nosy, so he didn't ask. Gemma had filled him in about Scarlet after her ordeal on the cliff.

'I've *never* seen her so . . . messed up', Gemma had said. 'She was as white as a ghost and trembling like mad. I was pretty worried for a while, but she told me all about it and by the time she'd finished she seemed a whole lot better. The best thing is that it frightened her so much she's completely changed her mind. Last night we went to see Mrs Woods, and she and Scarlet talked heaps. We ended up all saying prayers together, and Scarlet's become a Christian. Jarryn, isn't that great?'

This had been news indeed, and Jarryn wondered how much of this Tank knew. If he knew all of it, then that would explain much of his quietness today. If he knew nothing of it, then what did he and Scarlet talk about this morning? Poor Tank, thought Jarryn, he really wasn't having a very good time on this camp. And to make matters worse, from Tank's point of view, thought Jarryn, the first girl he'd ever really taken more than a passing interest in goes and turns Christian on him! If he didn't know how seriously that could affect Tank, Jarryn would have laughed.

After turning off the main track, they followed the convoy along a two-wheel depression in the grass over a rising plain toward the base of two enormous hills. When they could go no further, everyone got out and began to climb down into the creek bed itself. Except for a happy trickle which sprinted merrily over rocks and around boulders at the very bottom, it was dry. Huge slabs of red granite stepped upwards on either side as Tank and Jarryn made their way along the creek bed toward a shoulder of hillside which created a turn. Lizards sprang in alarm and blinked into crevices or beneath boulders, dragonflies skimmed and hovered over the less mobile pools, and tadpoles, huge and fat, wriggled about lazily in the shallow water.

Beyond the turn they came to the dam. Obviously built by hand, it spanned the rough U-shape formed by the creek bed. It was made entirely from slabs of the surrounding granite, without a skerrick of cement. At its deepest, the wall stood a little over two metres high and was evidently quite thick, as three or four people were already walking along it without any apparent need to watch their balance. A loud splash from the other side satisfied Jarryn's silent curiosity about whether it held water.

It turned out to be very nearly full. This side of winter it had been collecting and storing water for a good while, and since the weather had not been especially hot until now, there hadn't been much evaporative loss. It looked deep and clear and inviting as it rippled softly against the wall. Along the edges, red granite wobbled invitingly below the surface like warm red-golden steps into a rich person's swimming pool. Beyond where the natural rise of land rose from the water, Jarryn could see the creek bed divide. The dam was fed, apparently, not by one, but by two waterfalls.

'I might have a swim', he declared, pulling off his T-shirt.

Tank looked at him, and then at the water. Suddenly he grinned. 'Yeah, why not?'

They stood on the wall, feeling their backs warmed by the sun and fending off friendly taunts from everyone. It was plenty deep enough, but who was going first?

'Go together on three. I'll count', Scarlet called. Gemma smiled; she had felt the water.

'One . . . two . . . THREE!' They both jumped, Jarryn straight in, but Tank, calculating and after three quick strides along the wall, rolled himself into a ball and delivered a bomber right in front of Scarlet and Gemma, wetting them both thoroughly.

There were loud screams and gasps and howls of laughter. The water was *freezing*!

Jarryn, gasping at the shocking coldness, shook the water from his hair and looked around for Tank.

'You'll pay for that, Tank. You just watch your back from now on. You're really going to pay for it', Scarlet scolded with a grin.

'That goes double', Gemma added, her jeans and the bottom part of her shirt dripping still from the recent spray. Tank's grin broadened as he turned and swam back to Jarryn.

'Too cold in here. I'm getting out', he said. Jarryn joined him.

In spite of flashes of good humour, especially when Scarlet was around, Tank still lapsed into long stretches of silence throughout the afternoon. They explored the two waterfalls,

71

climbing up one, walking across the top shoulder of the mountain, and then coming back down the other. They had skimming competitions with several other youth-group members to see who could make a sliver of granite skip the most times across the dam, with bonus points for making it leap over the wall as well, and they caught tadpoles by the dozen to race them down a slippery stretch of black slimy rock over which the water slid on its way to the dam below.

Tank felt what seemed to be a great weight pressing in on him from all around. For what seemed to be enormous lengths of time he found himself brooding about Scarlet and the complete turnaround she had made after just one, admittedly frightening, episode on a cliff face. She should have been over that by now, surely? But there was a change in her. Not that he had really known her well enough to compare in the first place, but the change was so marked that he could see it, sense it somehow. Scarlet was *different*! Why? Because she was a Christian now? She still stirred, joked, and mucked around.

When he caught himself brooding like this, he made a conscious effort to snap out of it. He didn't really feel like grinning or joking and enjoying himself, but he felt even less like answering questions about what was wrong with him. The truth was, he didn't know.

To Tank, the afternoon seemed to drag along at half speed. It took forever for the sun to give in and start heading west, for the youth-group campers to make for their vehicles and set off back to the shearers' quarters and tea. Then for some reason that he couldn't afterwards remember, he and Jarryn were the last to go.

All up, Tank figured this was probably the longest, most frustrating, horrible day he'd had for a long, long time. The quicker they got back to camp the better, he decided.

Hoping to speed things up, Tank chose to drive. Jarryn said nothing and climbed into the passenger side of the Landcruiser, digging behind his seat for a jumper he had stuffed there earlier. Tank took off, the wheels spitting sand and grit behind them, quickly catching up with the convoy and following until they left the grassy track and moved onto the dirt road. Here the dust thrown up by the vehicles in front was so fine and powdery and thick that Tank had to drop back. Billows of red dust blew back toward them, not just from the vehicle immediately in front of them, but from all the vehicles in front of that too. The track came toward them from exactly the same direction as the breeze, and visibility was nothing but a red blur.

'This is hopeless!' Tank muttered, straining to peer through the dust and slowing down even more.

'We could stop for a while', Jarryn suggested. 'If we aren't careful, we might run into someone.'

'Surely there'll be a bend in the track soon; the breeze will blow the dust out of our way then', Tank said hopefully.

Jarryn shrugged. He didn't know how many turns there were in the track, or even whether it turned at all. He did know that it eventually returned to the shearers' quarters where they were camped, but that was all.

Tank slowed again and changed down a gear, crawling along at a ridiculous speed. Gradually the oncoming cloud of dust seemed slightly less mobile, just a little less dense, lighter. Ahead, the convey drew steadily away, the dust a long swirling train billowing and rolling like storm-clouds on a video with the fast-forward button on. Then it swirled and seemed to give up, stretched outwards and upwards, thinned and diluted, and then dissipated in a red cloud over the surrounding grass.

As long as they kept a good distance from the car in front of them, there wouldn't be a problem, Tank thought.

Late afternoon became early evening. Red and orange sunlight rested huge hazy shafts of light against the trees, the breeze freshened, and the taller mountain tops on their right darkened into silhouettes. There were rabbits everywhere, rabbits, sheep, emus, and mobs of kangaroos.

Teatime, Tank thought to himself. All the animals were out looking for food, and who could blame them? He was starving.

Ahead, the other travellers were still gradually pulling away. The angle of the road was changing, not enough to warrant catching up again, but enough to give Tank and Jarryn an outside view of the convoy across the curve in the road.

Tank confronted some of his frustration again. The day had been a miserable one for him. In spite of the fact that Scarlet wasn't angry with him, he felt that there was something unresolved. And tomorrow was the last day of camp. Scarlet would go back to Coffin Bay and probably become the best Christian this side of the black stump. What on earth had got into her?

He tried to imagine what it must have felt like, hanging on to that cliff like that, believing — *truly* believing — that he was going to die! It wasn't easy to imagine. He'd been scared on the cliff, yes, but more thrilled by it.

That wasn't working. So when was the last time he'd been really, really frightened? *That* was easy: when an ostrich had charged him out of the sheep-yards back near his farm. He'd been really frightened then. He tried to imagine how it would feel being locked in a room full of angry ostriches, or in the back of a semitrailer with no way he could climb to safety, no doors he could open, nothing he could put between himself and the birds, nothing he could hide behind. It wasn't difficult then to imagine how quickly the fear would build. Just the thought of it made his skin prickle. He agreed with himself that if he was put into a situation like *that*, there was a good chance that he would panic. Different things got to different people. But would it make him feel any differently about God?

Tank didn't know. He didn't know if he even believed that there *was* a God. He did know that everyone — or at least 99 per cent of everyone — he knew who went to church was either a wussy, a dork, or old, and no way known did he want to be any one of those.

But Jarryn wasn't any of those things. Neither was Scarlet, although since she was such a brand-new Christian maybe the wussiness hadn't rubbed off on her yet. And Steven, the speaker for the camp, he wasn't a dork either, far from it. What had Scarlet said about going to hell? No-one would save her because she hadn't let them.

Hah! Who believed in hell, anyway? That was just something parents told kids to make them behave! The thought of the devil prodding him into fiery torments was so weak that Tank nearly dismissed the whole line of thought with a laugh — except that two things happened.

The first was that Jarryn grabbed the dashboard and yelled to him to watch out for the kangaroo which suddenly lumbered out in front of the Landcruiser. It stopped there, in the middle of the road, watching them interestedly. Tank hit the brakes, and felt the wheels grab, then slide on the gravelly surface of the road. Although they hadn't been travelling fast, the momentum was still too great to stop them in time. Desperately Tank swung the wheel to the left. Along the roadside were some mallee trees and bushes, but between these, some clearer patches. Hoping to avoid hitting any more than a shrub or two, Tank hauled the Landcruiser over. It was a desperate attempt, but it seemed to work. The vehicle climbed up out of the depression of the track and, felling shrubs before it like a lawn-mower through long grass, bounced violently to an uneven, uncomfortable halt some ten metres off the road.

Tank and Jarryn looked back. The kangaroo still sat there, in the middle of the road, watching them. Then, almost as if it had shrugged, it hopped leisurely off into the scrub on the other side.

The second thing happened as Tank flopped back in his seat and closed his eyes. He hadn't had time to be frightened; his reactions had been purely instinctive. Why was it, then, that his mind, reverting back to his previous line of thought as though nothing had interrupted it at all, suddenly chose to show him a picture of the devil prodding him with his pitchfork, not into a fiery furnace, but into an empty room full of angry ostriches?

Chapter 8

Of all the things to happen, this was the cherry on the icing, Jarryn thought. 'Dumb kangaroo!' he exclaimed as he shoved the door with his shoulder, swinging it open.

Tank unwound his window and let himself out by levering the outside door handle. Carefully they walked around the Landcruiser, checking the tyres and investigating the ground they'd covered before finally stopping. It was pretty rough. They'd flattened a few shrubs, bounced over several miniature mountain ranges, and come to a halt in a sort of ditch.

'Doesn't look like we've done any damage', Jarryn said hopefully. 'There's nothing along here high enough apart from those bushes we flattened back there.'

Tank shook his head. He was so angry that he couldn't trust himself to speak. It was yet another frustration added to his already miserable day. Reaching into the back, he grabbed the water container and took a long drink. The ice had melted long ago, and the water was barely cool.

'You want to back it out?' Jarryn offered.

Tank shook his head. 'No, you can do it', he said.

Jarryn climbed in and twisted the key. The motor turned but wouldn't start. He tried again. After a third time he stopped. 'There must be something wrong with it. It never plays up unless it's cold.'

Tank undid the bonnet and lifted it, peering inside. 'Try it again', he said. Jarryn did so.

Still the motor turned but wouldn't start, yet nothing looked out of place or damaged.

'I think I know what the problem is', Jarryn said then, climbing out and coming around to where Tank was. 'According to the fuel gauge, we're out of petrol.'

Tank looked at Jarryn. They had checked the fuel just before leaving Stone Dam, and it had been three-quarters full. That could only mean one thing: they had holed the petrol tank! Both boys seemed to come to this conclusion together. Dropping to their stomachs, they peered underneath the Landcruiser. Immediately they could smell petrol, and Jarryn wondered why they hadn't smelt it before.

'Now we're really stuck', Tank said, as if it was another item to be added to the long list of ills against him.

'We'd better see how big the hole is. Maybe we can plug it with something . . .' Jarryn began as he wormed his way underneath.

Although it was pretty dim there, it was easy to see the hole. It was as big as a kettle, and the splintered stump of one of the shrubs they had flattened was still wedged inside it, twigs, branches, and broken trunk still connected. It seemed to Jarryn that as they had landed after one of the more 'springy' bumps that had catapulted them, the force of it had uprooted the shrub. It had probably rolled underneath, and then been driven into the fuel tank as they had met with the next obstruction, a mound of dirt or another shrub perhaps.

Grabbing a spike of wood that protruded from the jagged, gaping hole, Jarryn wriggled it. Inside the tank there was little corresponding movement, but it was obvious that beyond the opening, which looked as if it had been hit with a crowbar to get it started and then finished off with a giant can-opener, quite a sizeable piece of stump was well and truly wedged there. No wonder they had no fuel! There was no question of plugging it.

'We can't fix this', he told Tank. 'The hole's just too big.' He began to worm his way back from under the vehicle.

For Tank, this was the last straw. Turning away from the Landcruiser, he stormed off, trailing a stream of curses behind him. He kicked out at everything, he picked up rock after rock and pelted them at a tiny nearby shrub until he had stoned it to pieces, and then he came back to the Landcruiser, kicked the tyres, opened and slammed the door twice, and sat down, hot, sweaty with exercise, and still no calmer.

Jarryn, who had watched all this from where he sat against the front wheel, said nothing. There was no sense in trying to talk to Tank while he was like this. Better to keep out of it. But Tank didn't allow that.

'What do we do now?' he demanded, getting up again and beginning to pace up and down.

'Wait, I suppose', Jarryn answered. 'Someone will come back for us eventually.'

'Eventually! I could starve before then!' Tank exclaimed, and Jarryn had to grin.

'Well, they won't look for us until they're sure we're not just doing some extra sight-seeing . . .'

'Great! So what should we do, start walking? You're the man with all the ideas. What do *you* do when you don't want to be somewhere and you've got no choice?'

Jarryn wondered if Tank meant more by that comment than just today's situation. Was he blaming Jarryn for being out here in the first place, on this camp? Jarryn felt uncomfortable.

'Well?' Tank said again. Clearly he expected Jarryn to say something.

'Um . . .' he said, 'pray, usually'. It was risky saying that, but it *was* the truth.

Tank threw up his arms. 'Marvellous!' he said, black exasperation flowing from him like oil. 'What good is that going to do?'

Jarryn looked at his friend for a moment. 'It does a whole lot more good than you think. I've been praying for you for weeks, and it's got you here . . .'

Tank's expression was explosive. 'You needn't have bothered . . .' he said.

'. . . and it got Scarlet safely back from abseiling, *and* saved you a heap of trouble explaining things . . .' Jarryn continued.

Now it was Tank's turn to feel uncomfortable. 'Yeah, well, if God gave me ideas like he gives you, I'd go to church too.'

'He doesn't just give me ideas, not the way you mean. He reminds me of things I've already learnt. Sometimes they're things I can use. Sometimes I don't get any ideas at all. Anyway, what have you got against praying? You've never even tried it, so how can you say it doesn't work?'

'It's stupid . . . talking when no-one's there . . . You look such a dork.'

'So do you when you go mad cheering at the footy', Jarryn returned quickly.

Tank pelted another stone at a wattle bush, showering leaves from its branches like gumnuts in a high wind. Then he threw back his head and looked up at the sky, yelling in a loud voice: 'Hey, God, give me some of those ideas like you give Jarryn so we can get out of this'. He turned then to see what effect this was having, but all Jarryn did was grin and say: 'You forgot to say amen'.

'Didn't work, anyway', Tank grumbled. They were at a stalemate, and Tank suddenly had no anger left in him. He reached into the back of the Landcruiser for the water bottle again, offering it to Jarryn first. Jarryn shook his head.

Now that the sun was nearly set, the evening air was cold. Although his anger had disappeared, Tank was still restless, unable to sit down and just wait. It would be totally dark soon, and if anyone did come back looking for them they wouldn't see them this far off the track without some sort of beacon to attract attention. Kicking a patch of ground till it was bare of grass, Tank set about building a fire. Jarryn didn't help with the fire, but he did scout around until he found two squarish granite rocks which could be used as seats. By the time he had lugged them back and put them in place, Tank had a supply of dead wood piled up. Carefully he poured a tiny amount of petrol from the jerry can onto his handkerchief, screwed it up so that the fluid soaked through into the material, and then stuffed it under some kindling. Next he put an old biscuit wrapper from under one of the Landcruiser's seats onto the kindling and covered the whole lot with twigs. He lit the biscuit packet and stood back to watch as the flames crept along the plastic paper toward the kindling. When they reached the handkerchief there was a soft rush of flames as the petrol ignited and the fire burnt up with gentle vigour, catching the twigs alight in no time. Finally Tank sat down.

There was nothing left to do, then, but watch the fire and occasionally throw on some extra wood. The evening grew cooler, and from time to time either Tank or Jarryn had to go off in search of more branches to burn.

Tank stared at the Landcruiser. The bonnet was still up from their initial investigation into why it wouldn't go. By the front tyre stood the jerry can, still brim full. There was enough fuel there to get them all the way home, let alone just back to camp. Frustration niggled at Tank's insides. If only he could use that fuel!

The sky was again sparkling clear, with a brilliant semi-full moon and masses of stars. The temperature still dropped; another frost by morning, Tank thought. Again his eyes swung to the jerry can. What a pain — fuel just waiting there to be used . . .

He stood up and moved to the Landcruiser, rummaged around behind the seat, and dug up the spotlight. Connected to the battery, it threw a puddle of light onto the engine and, climbing onto the bumper bar, Tank looked down into it thoughtfully.

'What are you doing?' Jarryn asked as he came to join Tank.

'Just fiddling', Tank answered.

Jarryn looked down into the motor. He wasn't much into mechanics. Computers were far more interesting. He knew how to drive and where to put the fuel, oil, and water, and how to change a tyre, but that was all. Tank was different. He often messed about with the ag-bike at home and fiddled with things in the Landcruiser, but Jarryn couldn't see how it would do them much good now. Once you had a hole in the fuel tank, you were stuck, stopped, and stationary as far as he was concerned.

Peering down into the motor, Tank traced the fuel line from the petrol supply underneath through to the fuel filter. The pipe changed from metal to rubber here, with a little clip to help seal the join. From the filter the pipe continued some 30cm to the fuel pump.

Tank looked from the fuel pump to the jerry can. If the pump sucked fuel from underneath the car, upwards to the motor, then maybe it could suck fuel from the jerry can! All he needed was some more hose.

Jarryn wandered back to the fire. If Tank was fiddling with motors, at least he was occupied.

If tank had been at home he would simply have cut a length from the garden hose, but out here there was no garden hose handy. Sighing, he stared at the motor. He really felt that this would work, but he needed some extra pipe. How much? he wondered.

He got down from the bumper bar and reached for the jerry can. It was heavy, but Tank hauled it up anyway and jiggled it down into a bit of space behind the battery and over the steering column. If the hose from the fuel filter, once disconnected from the main fuel line, was long enough to reach into the jerry can, they might even be able to get going.

Tank undid the little clip that held the rubber and metal fuel pipes together, and gently lifted the filter upwards. The hose just reached the rim of the jerry can, but that was all. Just a bit more hose, and they'd be right. Tank stood back and studied the motor. One lousy piece of pipe, that was all he needed!

And suddenly he saw it! The overflow pipe from the radiator was positively smiling at him.

'You little beauty', he muttered, as he set to work pulling it off the radiator and slipping it inside the pipe to the fuel filter. Using the clip which had sealed the join to the original fuel line, Tank now sealed the makeshift pipe and measured the distance to the jerry can. It was more than enough.

He was about to put the hose into the jerry can when another idea struck him. Quickly he went to the steering wheel and swung it back and forth. His suspicion had been right: the jerry can, where it sat now, interfered with the steering. Disappointed, he sat back to study the situation again.

The main problem lay in finding somewhere for the jerry can to stand. It had to be *in* the motor somewhere because the length of pipe wasn't enough to reach anywhere else, and the only other place it could go was on the other side of the battery, on the shock absorber mounts and the radiator support. But would the extension hose still reach?

He set to work to find out. Part of the task meant first moving the battery over. After that, there was a lot of jiggling, rocking, and turning to get the jerry can to sit as low as possible. Then came the acid test.

Lifting the extended pipe from the fuel and pulling it gently upwards, then looping it backwards, Tank found that it still reached nearly halfway down into the jerry can. For the first time in what felt like ages, he felt a surge of hope. Suddenly he wanted to achieve this, make it work, and get back to camp before anyone set out to look for them. But there were still a couple of hitches.

The jerry can lid would have to be off to allow the pipe in; how was he to stop dirt getting in and fuel from splashing out all over the motor? How could he stop the makeshift pipe from sliding out too, and how was he to hold the bonnet down with the jerry can still sitting where it was?

They were really minor problems compared to what he had already achieved, though, and Tank wouldn't be beaten now. First of all he used his T-shirt, stuffing it around the pipe and into the neck of the jerry can, both to hold the pipe in place and to prevent splashes. Then, carefully, he lowered the bonnet. It sat level as a table across the jerry can, but drooped downwards on the passenger side. Tank found that he could just get the hook on the passenger side done up. The bonnet held, secure enough not to blow upwards, and tight enough to hold the jerry can secure as well.

Excitedly, he disconnected the spotlight, sprang into the driver's seat, and turned the key. The motor groaned once, twice, and then suddenly roared into life.

Jarryn turned in amazement to see Tank's grin, wide and white in the moonlight, and Tank felt a marvellous surge of triumph at the look on Jarryn's face. He turned on the headlights and began to crawl carefully in a half circle, back toward the track. Quickly Jarryn busied himself putting out the fire, and within five minutes they were on their way back to camp.

Chapter 9

A search party was being organised as they drove in. Scarlet and Gemma ran to the Landcruiser, closely followed by Andrew, Steven, and a trail of others.

Quickly, and each unable to suppress a grin, Tank and Jarryn explained what had happened. Andrew unhooked the bonnet and appraised the makeshift fuel tank with admiration.

'Well, there must have been some divine guidance in that', he said. 'I don't know of many adults who would have thought of that, let alone someone who doesn't even have a licence yet!'

'He was hungry', Jarryn explained.

Tank grinned. 'Speaking of food, is there any tea left . . .?' he asked. Everyone laughed, and Steven told them that there was probably something left in the kitchen. By the time they'd eaten tea, both Jarryn and Tank found they were ready for a good night's sleep.

Tomorrow the camp finished. Tomorrow Scarlet went home, Tank thought, and even though his previous black mood had been relieved by his recent success with the Landcruiser, Tank could not, still, accept *why* she had chosen to become a Christian. She had been as strongly against it as he had the first day of the camp. It just didn't make sense.

'Come for a walk?'

Tank turned to see Scarlet, rugged up against the cold and smiling. Suddenly stuck for words, he looked at Jarryn.

'Not me', Jarryn said. 'I'm going for a long hot shower and bed.'

He shrugged. 'If you like', he said to Scarlet. 'Where to?'

'How about we walk to the creek bed?'

'OK.'

They walked in silence for a while. There didn't seem to be much to talk about. In fact, Tank, highly conscious of the silence, ran questions and comments continuously through his mind in a search for something useful and worthwhile to say. He dismissed everything and said nothing.

The creek bed, when they reached it, actually had moon shadows in it, but no water. It was quite deep, up to about two metres, and sometimes it was four or five metres wide. The bottom was sandy, mixed with fine gravel in places where water had raced around a curve and deposited the heavier granules in a risen shelf. Sandy ripples marked wide water places, and deep channels grooved where faster moving water must have raced.

For a while they wandered along the creek bed itself. Sometimes a rabbit would scuttle away, and once or twice a single bird call searched the plain for an answer. Scarlet walked to an old tree trunk that looked as if it had been washed up long ago, and sat on it. Tank sat beside her.

'How will you get home tomorrow?' she asked.

'Probably ring Jarryn's people and tell them what happened, and then go with the set-up like it is. If we don't turn up in a reasonable time, they'll come and get us', Tank told her.

'Doesn't it bother you, breaking down, I mean, and being stuck somewhere?'

'It did this afternoon. I was so wild. It's not scary, though, just annoying.'

'I think it was great you coming up with that invention like that. Are you brainy at school?'

Tank was surprised and pleased at this, and a little embarrassed. 'No, not really. Just average, I guess. Yesterday and today . . .' he paused a moment. '. . . I was feeling pretty . . . stupid, after what happened.'

'What happened was the best thing that could have happened to me', Scarlet said carefully. Tank remained silent.

'I guess I've sort of let you down . . .' Scarlet continued hesitantly. She really didn't know how he was taking all this, and she was feeling just a bit scared. Tank made it worse by still not saying anything.

'I'm sorry if I *have* let you down. I didn't do it on purpose. I just didn't have any choice.'

Tank still said nothing. He was trying to calm down a huge river of feelings inside — anger, irritation, guilt, excitement, and lots more that he couldn't even identify. Scarlet's last sentence froze him, though. No choice, she'd said. Of course she'd had a choice!

'There's always a choice', he said at last.

'Yes, but they're not all the right choices. I didn't become a Christian because I *felt* like it. Even when I did become one, there were feelings inside me that didn't *like* it. I guess I'm going to have to look at those one day. I became a Christian because . . .' She paused here. She hadn't actually worked this out for herself yet, let alone try to tell it to anyone else. '. . . because I was scared of what the alternative might be', she finished simply.

Tank's face grimaced in the moonlight. 'You mean hell?' he asked.

'Not the fire and brimstone one, although that did cross my mind on the cliff', Scarlet laughed, but then she was serious again. 'Mrs Woods says the *real* hell is much worse than that! She told me the world's a mixture of good and bad. But if God was to leave and take all the goodness in the world with him, hell is what would be left. Can you imagine what it would be like without anything *good* at all? That's what hell will be, complete separation from God and everything good. So I guess I'm still scared of going somewhere I'll hate, but for a different reason.'

'You might not go anywhere! It might just be . . . pop, lights out . . . and nothing else ever', Tank suggested.

'It might, but I'm not risking it', she told him.

'So you'll go to church and talk to thin air and spend the rest of your life scoring up goody-points, just in case?' Tank couldn't stop himself from saying it. He could even hear the bitterness in his own voice, and squirmed because of it.

Scarlet looked at him, surprised. 'Is that how you see it? But it's not like that at all.'

'How would you know? You've only been one for a day or so.'

'Well, Jarryn doesn't look like he's starved for fun. Does he score up "goody-points"? He doesn't seem that sort to me', Scarlet pointed out.

'Yeah, but he's different', Tank said.

'Different? How?' she asked.

Tank squirmed. He'd been backed into a corner, and now that he really had to do some hard thinking he was finding that his usual answers didn't hold water. In fact, Jarryn hadn't really changed all that much at all. He was still the same Jarryn, only somehow more so, if anything. And he *didn't* set out to score up goody-points either, Tank had to acknowledge. People just liked him anyway. 'I dunno', he shrugged, just a tiny hint of irritation slipping through.

Scarlet changed the subject. 'Well anyway, I didn't want us to argue. I wanted to ask you something.'

'What?'

She looked down at her hands, lacing and unlacing her fingers, almost as if lost for words. After a moment she spoke. 'Well . . . I was wondering if we could . . . write to each other?' she said.

Tank took a moment to absorb what she had just said. 'I guess so, if you want to. I'm not very good at it, but if you write first I promise I'll answer it', he said. Secretly he loved the idea.

'I'll get your address from you tomorrow, then. Don't let me forget, will you?' she said. 'I think we should head back now, anyway. I told Gemma I wouldn't be too long.'

Tank stood up, and on a sudden impulse which he couldn't understand himself acting on at all, he held out his hand. Scarlet looked up at him, smiled, and took it. Together they walked back to camp.

There were no programmed activities for the following day except one massive pack-up and clean-up. Jarryn drove to the main homestead a kilometre away and phoned his parents so that they could come looking if he and Tank didn't arrive home within a reasonable time.

Once again Scarlet's group was rostered to clean the showers and toilets. People buzzed everywhere, trailers were hooked up, swags rolled, food repacked, belongings checked, rooms checked, and vehicles checked until at last everyone was satisfied that they had everything. Then, everyone was saying goodbye, getting into their vehicles, and moving out.

Someone had topped up the jerry can fuel tank from their own supply to make sure that the level didn't drop below where the overflow pipe reached; and armed with another full jerry can from Steve, Jarryn and Tank set off.

They travelled in silence, each thinking his own thoughts, watching the mountains, the heat shimmer above a rise in the road ahead, and an eagle, just a speck in the sky soaring overhead.

Jarryn drove, keeping to a steady pace to conserve fuel. Tank had been pretty quiet to begin with last night, after coming in from his walk, but he had mentioned that Scarlet wanted to write to him. Jarryn had stirred him about it until Tank, laughing, had thrown his sneakers at him, then dodged away to go for his shower before Jarryn could take aim and throw them back. It had almost been like old times, Jarryn thought. So close; yet there was still this unspoken, unbreachable barrier between them — always this *thing* about him being a Christian.

Tank gazed out at the incredible countryside around him. He realised how lucky he was to live this close to the ranges, to be able to reach them, go camping, have a mate like Jarryn and a girl like Scarlet who wanted to write to him. He thought about the camp, how he hadn't wanted to go. It had been a camp of extremes, some really great things, and some absolutely awful; but it had made him think a lot.

After going through the Dog Fence gate, Jarryn decided it would be a good idea to check the fuel. While Tank shut the gate behind them, he lifted the bonnet and began pulling out the T-shirt that held the make-do fuel line in place.

Tank came around to the front of the Landcruiser. 'Is it OK?' he asked.

'Yes, but I reckon we should top it up, anyhow. The lower it gets, the more it sloshes around in there as we drive.'

Tank nodded, and went to get the spare jerry can.

'That was a pretty tricky idea, you know', Jarryn marvelled aloud as they got going again. 'I'd never think of doing that in a million years.'

'That's only because you don't like engines much. It wasn't so great really, not like your winch thing.'

Jarryn laughed. 'That's not my idea. I told you, I got that from the Leyland Brothers on TV.'

'Yeah, but it worked.'

'So did yours.'

'And I didn't even pray', Tank grinned, stirring.

For a split second Jarryn was so surprised that he had no reply. Then suddenly he grinned in return.

'Yes, you did', he crowed. 'I heard you. "Hey God", you said, "give me some ideas like you give Jarryn".'

Jarryn's imitation was so startingly like Tank's mock prayer that Tank had to laugh. 'Yeah, but that doesn't count. It's not real', he said, dismissing it.

94

'Well, you got your answer anyway, real or not', Jarryn said.

There wasn't much Tank could say to that. He saw it one way, Jarryn saw it another. It was all a matter of choice, really.

They were nearly home. They had already turned onto the road which led through the sheep country that Jarryn's parents leased. But it was true, Tank thought, whether the prayer had been a real one or not, Tank *had* got an idea. One he was capable of coming up with himself, he knew that, but that was just what Jarryn had said; God used things you already knew usually. Did God speak with ideas and things that happened — like Jarryn's winch thing, like Scarlet's 'death', and his own stark imaginative picture of the devil prodding him into a room full of ostriches? And even as he thought, his own mind was already adding 'and connecting up a jerry can of fuel to the cruiser'!

Tank sat very still. If God had just spoken to him . . . Surprised, he found that he didn't automatically dismiss that. God *could* be real, Jesus *could* be real, and this Holy Spirit guy that everyone kept on about *could* be real too! Jarryn believed it, Scarlet believed it, Steve believed it! They weren't stupid, and they did seem to be quite adamant about the truth of it! Maybe he shouldn't be so hostile about it until he'd checked it out more.

Jarryn pulled up outside his front gate, switched off the motor, and stretched. He was glad to be home, and he was sure Tank would be. This camp had probably done the opposite of what he'd been praying for, Jarryn thought. To Tank, their differences must now seem irrevocable. Tank's stirring had proved as much as anything what he still thought about

Christians. Would he just start to drift away now, seeing less and less of Jarryn until they just weren't even friends any more?

Tank climbed stiffly from the passenger side and stretched as well. 'What are we doing tomorrow?' he asked.

'Don't know. Haven't thought that far yet', Jarryn replied. He reached into the Landcruiser and began hauling out swags and bags, dropping them onto the ground by the gate.

Tank wandered around to the driver's side door, opened it, and climbed in. When Jarryn had everything, he started the motor. 'I know I'm going to sleep like a log tonight', he grinned as he put the vehicle in gear, 'but I'll come back for a while after I've unpacked. I suppose I'll need to find out what time church starts next Sunday.'

Already he was letting out the clutch and moving. In the side mirror Tank could see Jarryn's surprised face, and laughed as he put his foot down and headed across the paddock for home.

Jarryn wasn't at all sure what to make of that, but he'd known Tank long enough to recognise when he was stirring and when he was not. And right now, even though Tank had laughed, Jarryn knew for sure that he was *not*.